## Dedication

Caroline Tann for pushing me forward,
and to Mrs Woodall for always encouraging
me to never stop writing

Eve Knightly

# TALENT SCHOOL. 1032

AUSTIN & MACAULEY

A CIP catalogue record for this title is
available from the British Library.


ISBN 978 1 84963 063 4


www.austinmacauley.com

First Published (2011)
Austin & Macauley Publishers Ltd.
25 Canada Square
Canary Wharf
London
E14 5LB


Printed & Bound in Great Britain

# Prologue

The world isn't like it used to be, things have changed and by changed I do not mean everyone is in snazzy silver jumpsuits and lives on the moon. No, if only it was that simple, you see the thing is that technology has advanced greatly over the past few years, as everyone predicted it would, and that is exactly the problem.

Picture a cold lab, situated in a high building, its glaring glass windows looking over a bustling city. The city beneath it is unimportant, the lab is not. In here there is a machine, but you can't see it, no one in the lab can. It is covered by a white sheet blowing from the creeping air in the vents. Two men are in this lab, one rubbing his temples as he slumps into a wheeling chair, his reddened eyes show his lack of sleep as well as his bristly chin and greasy hair. The other man is the complete opposite; his smile is tweaked into a grin and framed around his clean and shaven face. Briskly the man, clean and shaven, walked across the room and looked down to the unimportant city.

"The world is changing out there," he smiled.

"For the better or for the worse?"

"Now, now, Anthony don't be like that. These revelations that you've had over the past few years have finally come about, your work is being used and the benefits are…"

"Fatal," Anthony moaned.

"You miserable bugger, how can you say that? The research we've produced to make these machines, to finally have it come about, is amazing. Surely you must be certain of that?"

"I'm not particularly certain of anything at the moment, Richard. In fact, if there is something for me to be certain about it's that the more I learn about the world, the less I want to know."

"What a load of bull," Richard laughed. "This idea of yours has been genius from the moment you discovered the right brain connections, and to think I'm part of all of this."

"Giving knowledge to those who don't deserve it, separating talent from the rest of the world and into sub-categories among schools, it's bloody ridiculous."

"It's ingenious, those who have talent use it, those who don't get given knowledge to hold down a steady job that will benefit the country and furthermore, the world," Richard argued.

"It's bloody ridiculous, this isn't what I set out to achieve."

"Your first goal was too small, this… this is the big league."

Anthony stood up swiftly, the chair wheeling across the room and flying into the wall, barely missing the covered machine. Richard seemed shocked. "The goal was not small and if anything, should still be set out to be achieved. I wanted to produce a machine that would give knowledge to those who were unable to learn, not to those too lazy to do so or too knowledge-hauling to give a damn as to what's going into their greedy minds."

"And we will work on that goal, but for now, think of how this will help the world. Think of how it will further the advancement of the human race. The talents can entertain; the knowledge-filled can work…"

"And what of us?" Anthony stood over Richard, for a second he was afraid.

"Us?"

"Yes, Richard, us, the ones who have attained knowledge naturally by learning, the ones who will be outweighed by any knowledge that is fed to others by those… those things?"

His fear was soon brushed away by the thought of the future. "We will be the natural talents, the ones who have obtained from the very beginning. The ones who are the most intelligent, the ones everyone will look up to, the ones everyone will have to rely on. After all, someone has to fix the machines when they get broken, someone has to know how they work, that is us. And don't be so sharp in naming the machines, those *things* will help the human race and it all began with you, Anthony, you and me."

"I don't want this and you shouldn't either," he shook his head feverishly and muttered cursed words to Richard under his breath. When he looked up, his eyes were two red circles of wrath. "That's it, we call off the machines now, tell them they don't work."

"Don't be ridiculous, Anthony, we are going ahead with it, with everything."

"Tell me, Richard," Anthony bellowed. "Do you really think the plans are a good idea, really? Putting people who have 'natural' talent into separate schools away from everyone else and what is this all about natural talents; sports people, musicians, artists and writers, and are these even talents."

Richard wasn't a man to change his mind and during Anthony's speech, he had already thought up his own retaliation.

"After three years of getting it all planned, getting everything ready for action and allowing it to go ahead... I will not let you cancel this, we'll go down in history if we leave it, as the people who changed the world."

"Changed it for the better or worse? It's being called off." Anthony, his mind's decision made by his own terms of knowledge and not knowledge fed through his machines, bounded to the door in long, determined strides. Richard was quick to block his exit.

"Don't be stupid Anthony."

"My mind's made up Richard. Move."

"I won't let you ruin this for me, so many failed attempts and now you're going to let my success slip," Richard whimpered.

"Your success? I believe it was me who invented the machines, you were simply there at the time."

"You lying bastard, move one step and I'll... I'll..." Richard stuttered.

"You'll what? Wait for me to invent a weapon so you can use it against me?"

"I don't need any weapon of yours to kill a man."

"No," Anthony sniggered.

"No," and Richard was right, he didn't need any weapon made by Anthony to kill him. Because the gun from his coat pocket was enough to kill him without needing to steal anything. The only thing Richard was stealing from Anthony now was his last breath. But that was only in the lab, after getting rid of Anthony's remains, Richard would steal everything else from him as well. He would steal his ideas, he would steal his ideals and then twist them to make his own, and his own ideals would shape the world over the next 100 years, until those hundred years were finally forgotten and the machines were moulded even more to create false memories and eradicate them. Over the next hundred years, life would change into an onslaught of the weak and the very same people Richard had set out to help, and history would cease to exist as a new century is born. A new century where the people were separated and knowledge was law, and without it was death. Richard shot Anthony and the blood splattered across the wall, and onto the white sheets that covered the machine, the vents whipped up passing air and the sheets fell to the floor to reveal the machine that would change the world.

# Chapter 1

I am a writer, thank God for it, even if scientists are trying to prove that there is no such thing. I started writing in year 9 and found that I had a knack for it, then they labelled me as a jewel-child and took me to a special school. Thank God I noticed that I could write before I went into year 10, it was so close and all. I don't mind being in this place, this 'special school'. I'm seventeen now and I have been here for almost two years and I still don't mind. I thank God, if there is one, every day for giving me my talents and for letting me stay in here with naturally talented people, instead of out there with those knowledge-fed droids, those human robots. No, I would much rather be in here. I would much rather be in 'Talent School. 1032.'

There are over 1032 talent schools around the world; we were the last talent school to be made. They each hold up to one hundred students and no more than that. It is a boarding school, though it would be more accurate to call it a prison. We have all the essentials we need; shops, cinema and other things, however they are all inside the walls of the talent school and we are not allowed out. Anyone who tries to get out is punished greatly under penalty of not wanting to benefit the changing world; I wish it would change, I wish it would change right back to the way it was. I don't think anyone can remember the history of what it was like, they have blotted it out so that it seems like this is the only future, present and past and because of this, we don't know what year it is; they call it the new years and this is the 50th new year since those machines came and worked. If I ever find the men and women that created those monstrous machines I will kill them, not that I don't know who created them, their faces paint the news so often that it's not worth watching, but they are guarded heavily, seen as the true geniuses, like us jewel-children.

We do not have names here, we are forced to abandon our names when we leave for Talent School and though it would probably be more sensible to call us by numbers, they do not. We are called jewel-names, like sapphire and amber. Works well if that's already your name, well, not for me. My name here is Emerald 2.0 and my real name is Tanya. I don't call people by their jewel-names; I call them by the names they love, just like I love to be called by my real name, by some people anyway. I have short blond hair that goes from the back to a racing point that stops at the edges of my chin and I'm not small, but I'm hardly tall.

The school is separated strangely, they did not put the sports people with the sports or the artists with the artists, they separated them. We suspect it is to make our creativity flow, so that we do not break the rules as much and we don't get bored, and, of course, we are right. There are ten blocks, each with ten students; they try to have five girls and five boys, but sometimes it doesn't work out that way. It did for us though. In our block, which is the Copper block, we have five girls and five boys. The blocks are named after how talented they judge us to be, sometimes they can switch people round, for example, Ruby 3.1 went straight from the Tin block to the Gold block a few weeks ago. In our block we all try to stay at a certain level just so we can stay together, the higher we go the more money we are likely to make when we are older, but we're all fine here and in this block, plenty of money is to be earned. In our block there is me, Sugilite 9.8, Lace Agate 4.6, Lapis Lazuli 6.5, Malachite 1.2, Ruby 3.2, Jasper 6.7, Rose Quartz 2.3 Hematite 6.9 and Chrysocolla 3.8. The real names for these people are Sophie, Lucy, Luke, Malic, Ruby, Jasper, Rose, Henry and Chris. You may think it is strange that they have such names similar to their jewel names, but it is far from a coincidence. Our headmaster, Alec, he likes to be called, decides the names when we get here and tries to make them as close to ours as he can; for some, like Ruby and Jasper, it's alright. As for me, well, he decided on my name because of the colour of my eyes instead. He really is great, I think everyone would hate to have a new headmaster. He isn't old and cranky, far from it, he is twenty-four and looks younger every day, and he teaches everyone at some point in the week. One of the upsides to this institution is him, he makes the days worthwhile and thanks to him, I don't hate my jewel name because I am his emerald eyes. Lucky him though, he gets his own name. When you leave school, if they think your name fits then you can have it, that is, if you remember it and I am determined to remember mine, and I will not have it changed.

The school is very structured and we are given goals depending on what we can do, for example, if a person can sing then he or she must practise a song every week, then perform it. If a person can draw, they must complete at least four paintings a month. For me, I get a little longer, I have two months to create a new book. I have had seven of my books published out of twelve and right now, they are out there being read by drones. I don't mind writing; I like it, not to say that I would not write even if I hated it, anything's better than being a drone, even if I am in a prison. Even though I don't get paid for my books and all the money raised goes to funding whatever they want, I don't mind, at least it fills the drones out there with some emotion so that they don't become emotionless robots. I try and fill every page with emotion, my books drip with it and that is why they don't get published sometimes, they are said to be too emotional, but really those people out there need all the emotion they can get.

"Thank God it's Wednesday, if there is one."

Wednesday, my favourite day, and it is my favourite day because every Wednesday, five people from the Copper block sneak out to the outside world and enjoy what is there. We go to nightclubs and restaurants and watch how the drones individualise themselves, we sneak into places they work and places they play. I don't know why we do it, after all, if we were to get caught the punishment would be severe, yet we would still do it, even if we did get punished. Maybe it gives us hope, maybe it makes us think what is normal and what is not, who is to say; either way whatever the reason we still do it and we enjoy doing it.

"Got everything you need? Money, phone, map?" Henry said.

"Like I need a map," I choked. "I've been around that place hundreds of times. I know it better than the inside of here."

"Take a bloody map, will you?" Malic persisted like he always did. He was one of those very cautious people, him and Henry shared that quality and yet in everything else, they were

17

completely different. Henry was naturally smart without a machine, he was our techno guy and his dusty grey eyes could work out the notes for any piece, then his fingers could strum them, whereas Malic was a blond, pretty boy, taller with deep blue eyes, as any irresistible pretty boy should have, he could reach the high notes and the low notes, meaning that he had to look good or girls would really avoid him. We are all seventeen here, Chris is the oldest and he looks it with his hazel eyes and that strange hair, the hair that isn't orange but isn't brown, it's like a metallic red; I suspect that all artists have something strange about them, and this is his something strange.

"No, I ain't taking a map, I don't need it."

"Just take a map, Green Eyes, if you get lost it will be the death of all of us, especially me." Chris ushered, how poetic he was.

"Oh, fine," against my will I shoved the pocket sized map into my rucksack. "Damn, it bloody takes half my rucksack up."

"Right, back to the checklist, torch?" Henry started, always so prepared and organised.

"Check," the four that were going, including me, shouted, that is Malic, Lucy, Ruby and I.

"Pocket knife?"

"Like we ever use it, check!"

"Money?"

"You said that already," I grinned, "can we just go. If we don't go now, the Blue Ray club won't let us in."

"Not until I've finished my check list."

"Well, while you're here finishing your checklist, we'll be dancing in the Blue Ray club."

"Just let him finish Green Eyes."

"Fine," I huffed. Why was it that Chris could always control me? Not that I minded.

"I'm done now anyway, let's go then, bloody impatient."

"Oy?" I turned round and met Chris's red-tinged eyes, I could always smile when he gazed at me with his hazel-tinted eyes, sometimes it's as if his eyes alone were making me smile, all by themselves.

"Be careful," he smiled and sweetened it with a kiss.

"I always am." What a lie, I'm never careful, I almost got caught two weeks ago and the two weeks before that, but, of course, if I told Chris that he would worry, and him worrying is like a dagger through the heart.

The way out was through the floorboards in the girls room, which was quite annoying as when one group went out, they would wake up any people in that room when coming back. Lift up two floorboards and there's a hole down to the bottom, go down the ladder, then you have to walk twelve metres forward and then there is a grid, open up the grid, drop down and go through the hole that takes you under the restricting walls of the Talent School. You'll end up climbing up a ladder and out of a sewer in a back alley, not the nicest way to go but it took us a while to create the passage and it wasn't easy at all. When we get to the Blue Ray club, they'll check our identification by hooking us up to an ID machine via the back of our necks. This is where we are wired to the knowledge machines in school. Since we aren't old enough and are escaping temporarily from Talent School, we use extra adaption's which are like USB's that lie about our age and location when we're hooked up.

The Blue Ray club flashed its fluorescent lights, crashing waves of sound throughout the dancing people, they weren't drones here, they were people; dancing and music gave them free spirit, making them people and not drones. The lights had to keep to the colour of the name; they were all blue-making the place seem like a hazy wave or the depths of the ocean. It was gorgeous; you would never find entertainment like this in the Talent School. Beer was served and, of course, Lucy started to overdo it again, meaning we'd all have to carry her home again; she likes to go wild, I don't blame her, if I drank I would probably do the same. However, it is seeing people like Lucy react to the stuff that is specifically one of the reasons I don't drink it, it tastes ok but I prefer lemonade. I just wish Chris was here, I don't dance with anyone if he isn't here because I only want to dance with him. That means I will sit drinking lemonade and analysing the people and how they individualise themselves by means of clothes, jewellery, dyed hair, etc. To be fair, they do a very good job of it.

"Come and dance with me, Tanya," Lucy spat, swishing her drink from one side to the other. She really shouldn't drink so much, her and Rose need to practise a dance routine in the morning.

"If you put your drink down then, yes, I don't want anything spilling on this top,"

"Fine," she moaned and placed her drink into the hand of a stranger. She did make me laugh, good old crazy Lucy, I'm just glad that Rose isn't here as well; if she was we would have to carry two people home. Those two are two of kind, ebony and ivory, they can hardly be separated. Together they're like Henry and Malic, one singer and one musician that both make magic. I didn't mind dancing with her, after all, what else was I going to do and at least this way I can keep an eye on her. You have to keep at least a metre away though because she flails her arms out like crazy when she's drunk, letting that body-glitter make her tinted skin sparkle in the blue rays of light.

A boy, perhaps 19, began to swing his body in my direction, at first it was fine because I ignored him, but then, when his hands edged to my hips, I left the dance floor leaving Lucy swinging her arms as a defence.

"Lucy drunk again?" Malic laughed, and I could smell the heaviness of alcohol on his breath.

"And you?" I asked.

"I've drunk a few but I can hold down my gut, unlike Lucy." Lie, I thought, a few weeks ago when we went to Red Java he swigged so many drinks that he spewed all over the secret tunnel.

"Time is it?" he barked over the buzzing noise of swishing drinks and bumping music.

"It's about… shit…"

"What?"

"Damn it and God almighty,"

"If there is one," Malic said.

"It's already two."

"Damn checks are at half past, come on, where's Henry?"

"Last I saw he was talking to Ruby."

We searched the dance floor and bar with our eyes.

"And now he is making out with Ruby," he laughed and pointed to the blue sofa where Ruby and Henry were latched onto each other, "Oh God, he'll regret that in the morning."

"Come on!" I shouted, gripping Lucy by the arm and swinging her to the door.

"Aww, I was just getting started, wooooo," she howled.

"Shut up." I slapped her across the face; she had told me to do that if she ever got out of hand and I took every chance I could get to do so.

Malic came rushing over with Henry and Ruby stuck together like lichens on rocks; God, if there is one, he would curse himself in the morning for doing that, and Ruby would as well.

"Right, lets go."

It took us a while to get back to the grate, there were a few stumbles and a few tumbles and at one point, we had to scurry and hide behind the bins because the police were out on their nightly patrol searching for criminals or people who weren't supposed to be there, in other words, us. They weren't stupid, they knew that jewel-children tried to sneak out sometimes and it wasn't allowed, we knew that. It was a close call and when we broke through the two floorboards, we had to jump with our clothes on into our beds and pretend we were asleep, just in time. It was hard to get Ruby and Henry off each other and Lucy started pretending to snore, which I gladly slapped her across the face for again when the prefects came round.

Damn prefects, always up in our business, they aren't students like in normal schools. No, they're just people brought in to keep us in line, like they do a good job of that. In our minds prefect stands for Pretentious Ruling Extraordinarily False Ever Causing Trouble, but for short, we just call them pratfects, behind their backs, of course.

As soon as they were out of Copper block, Chris came into the girl's room followed by the rest of the lads and ladies.

"You were almost caught."

"We just lost track of time," Henry mumbled.

"You're supposed to be organised, Hematite," he always called us by our jewel names when he was mad. "What happened, Emerald?"

"Like Henry said, we lost track of time and would you rather us be caught by the police or by the pratfects?"

"Don't get angry with me, I'm not the one who was late."

"I'm not, Chrysocolla, but we almost got caught and it took us a while to get away, ok? Just leave it, we're back now so leave it."

"Fine, I'll leave it," Chris ended, meaning that we could all disperse. I had expected Chris to reach out and hold my hand, and I knew what was coming after he did so.

"Want to sleep in mine tonight?"

"Not tonight, I'm shattered."

"We could just sleep," he offered.

"I'm really tired and the beds are small."

"Well, I don't expect to be on one side with you on the other."

"I know, but…"

"Please, Green Eyes," he turned me round to face him and took hold of my other hand, "I was really worried about you, you were supposed to be back by half one, like always."

"Like I said we lost track of time."

"Were you dancing with anyone?"

"Just Lucy,"

"No one else?"

"Chris you know I would never... I only want to dance with you."

"I know, I'm sorry, I was just worried; you can sleep wherever, I'm sorry I pressured you, I just love you so much." Love, love, I don't know, I'm not sure if I can love, I loved my family but I had to leave them; even if I snuck out, they are at least three hours away from here. Love, no I'm not sure I can love you, Chris, not when you make me feel like this, so damned awful guilty, please stop it.

"And I've never loved anyone before..." Just stop it.

"But I love you and I love spending time with you..." Don't!

"But like I said, you can sleep wherever." I hate it when you do this and yet...

"Night, Tanya, I love you." I want to collapse in your arms; I want to drown in your gaze, please stop it. Whatever, whenever, fine, I agree, I will do whatever you want.

As he let go of my hand I took it again, and he smiled and led me to his bed. The bed was in the very corner of the room to the left and they had allowed him to graffiti his corner as much as he liked and so he did. It was covered with pictures and paint, posters and CD's glued onto the wall everywhere.

"Come on, then," I smiled, we didn't just sleep.


Lucy had the world's largest hangover in the morning, which is another reason why I don't drink, hangovers. She's lucky that

23

she doesn't have lessons on a Thursday, unlike Ruby and Henry who did nothing but avoid each other all morning. I suppose I shouldn't call them lessons, we get hooked to those machines for half an hour or so, then do a test on what we've 'learned', not really a lesson at all. I hate those machines; when you're on it you basically fall into a sleeping trance, which creeps me out, just thinking what they could be doing to us when we're in that trance, experiments of all kinds. I know a girl who woke up after going on one of those machines and that found a cut on her ankle afterwards, some say she already had a cut there but even so, I check myself fully after going on those things.

I didn't have lessons so, as always, I looked after Lucy for the whole morning, poor thing, though it really is her own fault.

"Feeling any better?"

"Yeah, I'll be alright. That's it, I'm never going to drink again." She said that two weeks ago.

"Of course you won't."

"I mean it this time."

"Of course you do."

"Tanya," she moaned.

"I've got to get back to my book, the deadline's this week and it's only one hundred and three A4 pages; I said it would be longer this time. I suppose I can drone out the love scene."

"What's it about?"

"You'll see when it's published, they always put it in the library."

"Spoilsport."

"Just rest," I said throwing the flannel in her direction and missing but not on purpose. I was a lousy aim.


I had promised at least one hundred and fifty pages; damn, why did I procrastinate so much. Let's see, there were the nights I went out on Wednesdays, meaning I wouldn't have done any work then because I would always 'prepare', at least, that's the excuse I use for doing nothing. I spent a lot of Thursdays with Chris, so I didn't do much then; I always kept the weekend free, except for those two weekends where we all went out on a big thing. Damn, I hope I'm not losing my touch. I've always been known for my punctuality and commitment, I always hand things in on time or before the date, I better not be losing my technique. If I have five dud books in a row they'll kick me out of this place. I'll be fine though, five books are very generous of them, I'm surprised. It's twenty dud pictures in a row for artists and ten dud songs for singers and musicians. It's different for sports people like Ruby, Sophie and Jasper, the sports are determined differently; we're not sure how that works.

One hundred and fifty A4 pages, not many to go. I need to add five scenes I left out, tag on the ending and extend the love scene, that should do it. "Loveless hope," why did I name it that, who cares, it's not like anyone cares about the name and besides, everyone likes things related with love, it is a heavy emotion after all. Damn it, I wish I could pay attention, sometimes it's so hard to focus these days, I'm losing my touch, damn!

"Screw this. I'm out for a walk, Lucy, back soon."

Why couldn't I pay attention, perhaps it's the rush from last night or maybe my mind doesn't want to think about stories anymore. I usually have so many ideas and yet lately, I've just been phasing out and not concentrating. I walked down the corridor that was close to the main office, which was where Alec worked most of the time. I hadn't talked to him for a while, lately I think my feelings for him are showing through and if Alec or Chris ever saw this, who knows what could happen.

"Emerald Eyes," I could recognise that sweet voice anywhere, whether it was in a night club, school, anywhere, it swirled with a heavy scent that left me woozy and sometimes scared, a man's scent. I stopped dead in my tracks.

"Emerald 2.0," I reminded him.

"No one's around, Emerald, come inside my office, I need to speak to you." Though he couldn't see, I was blushing a fierce red, I could feel it covering my whole body.

"Did I do something wrong, Sir?" I said as I sat down.

"When they are inspecting, I am Sir, when they aren't here I'm Alec, you know that. Why are you so tense lately?"

"Did I do something wrong... Alec?" It wasn't a particularly romantic name; in my books romantic names were Alonso and Alexandra or usually something foreign, and yet his name held a certain esteem that no other could, it suited him. He wasn't over-muscled but slender, not that I had seen under his shirt or any other item of clothing, but it seemed this way. His hair would always tiptoe over his forehead delicately as if it was afraid, but what was there to be afraid of? His smooth brown hair, his chiselling blue eyes or his masculine features. No he was perfect.

"No, nothing's wrong, I've just heard that you're not... having as much fun writing as you used to."

"It's not that, I just can't seem to concentrate very well. I used to like writing but my books... no one knows who writes them, I just want to be known."

"Don't we all Emerald Eyes, I wish I could get your name on those books but that kind of work is far from me. Have you finished the book for next Wednesday?"

"Nearly."

"It's not like you to leave it so late."

"I've been distracted and thinking a lot."

"Thinking? About what?" As I looked up he was smiling, smiling, such an adorable smile, such a tempting smile.

"Just things."

"If you don't want to share, it's fine." *No, I want to share, I want to share everything with you. I must be such a kid in his eyes, he's so mature, so understanding.*

"Thank you, I should go and get the rest of the story done."

"Good idea," he said leading me to the door, "and Emerald Eyes, don't think too much," he winked. He winked at me, what does that mean? No, it is nothing, I'm just over analysing things again.

"Did you hear?" Jasper laughed and Sophie joined in, obviously there was a joke that I wasn't getting and if it was about sports, I didn't want to know. So, because of this, I kept on doing my work as per usual, just a few more pages to go. However, the "Did you hear?" was obviously directed at me and so I looked up as they spoke.

"Oh my Gosh," Sophie would never say the Lords name in vain, if there is one. She was secretly very religious and kept a cross on a chain under her t-shirt at all times. It is a good job that they didn't get rid of religion, though they are trying to, or else Sophie would be lost. She prays at night, doesn't drink, smoke or do drugs and she has taken a vow of chastity, something that I would never be able to do now.

"Well," I said.

"I mean do you actually believe it, Sophie."

"I know they are terrible together."

"Well?"

"They've tried like how many times?"

"Seven."

"Well?"

"No, come on, less than seven."

"Ok, I think this is the third time."

"No way..."

"GUYS!" I blazed, "I have work so either tell me what it is, or leave."

"Ok, chill Tanya." Damn sports people, always seemed to be chilled, no bloody pressure, except to be amazing at sports.

"Well, anyway, you know Henry and Ruby were making out at the nightclub, according to you and Malic, though they denied it at first?" Jasper whispered, though I don't know why, no one was around. "Well, now they're together again."

"No! But they tried two times already."

"Yes, but apparently that kiss was amazing," Sophie giggled.

God, if there is one, they're back together again. I give it three weeks, I mean they have tried it before, they just don't compute like that and when they break up, we have to suffer the consequences because it makes the group really awkward.

Sophie and Jasper left together, I suspect that if there ever was to be a great couple, it would be them; they're the best of friends and they have so much in common. It's just that Jasper likes to tell stories about how he 'gets some' all the time and we all know he doesn't, but this scares Sophie meaning she just wants him as a friend. I keep telling him to stop it because I know he likes Sophie too. He is so annoying and stubborn sometimes, they all are. That's not important right now though, just twenty more pages to go and I'm done, should be easy, a week left before the deadline, twenty more pages.

It was done, just in time, too; it always got done in the end. No matter how much I procrastinated, it always got done and in some ways, that annoyed me. Sometimes, I consider not doing the work and seeing what the outcome will be like, a scolding most likely. Though the book was done and Alec smiled at me as I handed it in, I couldn't feel satisfied, not just because I knew, like all the other books I have published, that this book would never see a letter of my name on its cover, but also because in my bag there was another book I had with me; this I had been working on for the past five months and was one of the reasons why I had been procrastinating so much for the last few books I had to write. This book is perfect and I only wish that it could be published, I only wish it could see my name and it will. I am determined to get this book published with my name on the cover. Tanya Greyner it will read, and then things will change, then people will see. But how?

28

How do I get it published behind their backs and how do I get my name on the cover? I hadn't the slightest idea how to do this; I knew who would have a clear idea of who knows all about the publishing business, Henry, who knows about everything.

"What's on your mind?" For a minute I didn't hear Chris's rhythmic voice.

"Green Eyes?"

"Oh, sorry, I'm a little... I'm not sure."

"What's wrong?"

"Do you know where Henry is?"

"Henry, why?"

"I just need to find him." By this time we were walking down the corridor and Chris was getting irritated, he didn't like answers that weren't straight and were riddles, that's why he didn't read many of my books, not that I mind I suppose, they're not worth reading if you don't know who has written them. Chris, furious with the answers he wasn't getting, drove me to the wall, softly, but forcefully and pinned two hands either side of me so that I couldn't escape. First, he kissed me, that was his way of showing that he wasn't angry, just irritated and it was his way of making sure I wasn't scared. Sometimes, I was scared of him and kissing me full on the lips was his way of softening the fright. His kiss was long and hard, it was less softening my fright and more worsening it sometimes, and this was one of those times.

"Green Eyes," he stroked my hair away from my eyes, my face was focused on the distance and not him. "What's wrong?"

"I want to publish a book," I said honestly.

"You've published loads of books," he released me and we began to walk again.

"I mean I want to publish a book, one really amazing book that I've written, and I want it to be published with my name on the cover."

"What?" He stopped walking. "You can't do that."

"I knew you wouldn't understand," I walked on and didn't turn back and this was my way of controlling him; it didn't work most of the time but sometimes, it hit home and it hit hard.

"Wait, Tanya," he ran after me and I almost laughed at his predictability. "I do understand, I know it's hard and I want your name on those books as well."

"I need to find Henry," I demanded softly.

"He should have finished his tests by now, he'll be in the room," he said.


Henry was writing some new lyrics that needed to be in before next week and Malic was practising it, they were partners in singing.

"Worst piece you have ever written," Malic slumped, he always said that and then when it's done, he sings it and loves it.

"Go find someone else to write your bloody songs then."

"Maybe I will,"

"It'll be damn hard since your voice is like a dying cat."

"Millions of people have bought my singles."

"With my lyrics, with my chords."

"Pathetic details," Malic spat.

"Would you two shut up," Chris shouted and just like that, they did. After all everyone listened to Chris.

For a minute they stared at him, and then for another minute they stared at me as it was obvious that I was why he had so violently told them to shut up, they really did need telling to shut up a lot more often.

"I was wondering, Henry if, well I... I don't know how to put this..."

"For God's sake," Malic roared, he was in such a bad temper these days.

"If there is one," Henry added.

"Just spit it out," Malic hissed; like I said, a bad mood.

"Shut up, Malic," Henry defended me before Chris could speak; that's how *you* got on Chris's good side these days, you were nice to me, a rule that Malic didn't pay attention to.

"Henry," I began, about to swallow my words whole. "Do you know how to publish a book?"

Henry stared blankly at me before replying, "Depends, how they publish a book or how *you* can publish a book and why?"

"I want to publish a book, only I want my name on the cover."

The room fell silent, as I had expected it to do so. Malic stared at me with grinding eyes and an open mouth expression and Chris stood still. Henry however was thinking, the type of thinking he would do when considering something, in other words, I'm in.

"I don't know Tanya, it's risky dealings there."

"Please, I just want my name to be on the book, just one book,"

"They would most likely take it away immediately once they found out,"

"At least someone would know I wrote it, one person would know, they couldn't take it away that quickly."

"You'd be surprised."

I looked down to the floor, flopping my head and giving a heavy sigh, it often swayed boys, but not boys like Henry.

"I'll try and help you but if you get caught, I..."

"Didn't do a thing," I said.

He smiled and laughed, everyone here was so predictable.

# Chapter 2

Apparently books aren't hard to get into a store, a library; they're just harder to keep there. You could easily abandon a box of books in a store and the manager would place them on the shelves thinking they were legal merchandise.

The plan was this, Henry knew of a publisher, or rather a dealing publisher. He would edit it, print the copies and have them out in a week, for a price. I didn't think it was possible, but apparently it is. My name will be on the cover and it will be everywhere, and then maybe everyone will see what it is like and how things can change, maybe they will rebel against *them* and I will have started it all. It will go down in history, a history that will not be erased; I will go down in history and then everyone will know my name. That one book, that one book will have started it all and what a great book it is, an amazing spectacular book. The best I have ever written; "Shenray." It is my favourite and it will be everyone's favourite because it is the book of change. Piece-by-piece, this world we live in now will change and it will all be my doing, I will have done that and people will know; Tanya Greyner, the girl who changed life for the better.

When the book came out, I went out on a Wednesday night and we checked the library in the outside world, it was there and a day later it was gone. It had been in every book store, every library, everywhere and yet a day later, they all vanished and were replaced with the same book missing one crucial detail, my name. Apparently nothing was publicised, according to Henry, nothing was on the news about my name and from that I knew that somehow they had managed to get rid of anyone who saw my name on that cover. I just wish it could have been out for longer, I wish someone would have seen my name and remembered it, yet no one did and that is exactly what scares me. I flicked through the cover of 'Big Books' weekly magazine, my book was there but my name was not. Surely someone must have seen my name, it was all over the bookstores, there was even a big poster with the book and 'by Tanya Greyner' at the bottom of it in every shop window. I just can't understand why it wasn't acknowledged as amazing. That book is still out there though, they turned my book into a nameless piece like all my others and I'm going to change that. Tonight is a Wednesday and even if it is not my turn to go out, I'm going, I will show them. Rose said she would help and so did Chris, the others I didn't tell. We are going to hit every book store and library near here and write on the front cover of each book 'by Tanya Greyner', it is a good job the cover is pure white, it will make it easier to write on. Tonight is the night that changes history, tonight people will know, we have the right equipment and we have the knowledge of how; after all, we have done it before, it will be easy. By this time tomorrow everyone will know I wrote that book, everyone will know it was me and the future will be changed; I don't care what it takes but I will change it, I will.

"Ready to go?" Chris said.

"You sure about this?" Rose smiled at my anxious face, I was trying to look courageous but it just kept coming out as scared.

"Yeah, got the ski masks, just in case, security cameras and all."

"They'll know it's you, though, your name will be all over the books," Rose said, her frown deepening. "And there are other ways of identifying people now, remember they've got that new fingerprint up-close camera. We best not show any parts of our bodies or really any of our face either."

"I know, and listen you guys, if they catch me then it was all me, no one else, got that?"

Rose nodded, Chris didn't.

"Chris?"

"I'll go down with you Green Eyes. I agreed to this."

"No and don't disagree, if you do, Chris, I'll break up with you, you got that? So leave it." Then he did.

We split up as soon as we got out of the passageway to the real world, then Rose, Chris and I went to another grid on Twenty-Four Street. There we opened it up and went down into the sewers; from there we could get to the shopping centre quicker and there was a passage that went up to the library that we often used. We hit the shops first and got into all, but two, the heavily protected ones. In one we found a poster that had been used before with my name on it and so we put it up were it would be hard to get down, over the escalators. After the shopping centre, we went back down the grid and popped up into the library, sometimes the books were split up so we did the same and took a certain amount of sections each. Armed with my permanent marker I felt invigorated and dangerous as if the pen in my hand was a deadly weapon, and not just a fat stick with ink in it. I piled up some of my books that I had found, it was a big library so the books here were in masses, and then scribbled my name where it would be most visible. I stopped for a second as I could swear that I heard something, it wasn't a shuffling sound but a sound like sirens, police sirens, then when I listened again, the sirens had faded and I put the sound down to my imagination. When another sound met my ears I knew I had not imagined it; this time it was like the shuffle of feet, like a mouse tiptoeing across the floor, but I had still heard it.

"Rose?" No reply.

"Chris?" I hope to God, if there is one, that it's Chris and yet still no reply.

I went back to scribbling on my books and turned around to bring another one off the shelf. As I got up, I noticed a man and the book fell from my hand, he dodged and caught it then covered my mouth to stop me from screaming, this I did not expect. He gazed at the pile of books I had been scribbling on then leant down with my mouth in his hand, I crouched down too and he let go. I could have screamed, yet I didn't, when he placed his leather gloved hand over me I almost relaxed. I could not feel the hotness of his hand due to those cold leather gloves; they had to be leather because they were soft.

He picked up a book and eyed up the words written on it in the dim light, he smiled and looked me straight in the eyes, no sideway glances, no shudders, just straight in the eye. His eyes were like his facial features, barely visible and yet in the dim light, I could see that he had the most amazing eyes I had ever seen, eyes that only ever existed in books that I had so often written. They were a powdered ash-mauve colour and they relaxed me when I should have been scared. Slowly, he leant forward and at first I thought it was a dream, a dream where a mysterious man with beautiful eyes was about to kiss me; no, not a man, he wasn't as old as Alec, he was a bit younger, perhaps even my age. As his lips touched mine I jolted but did not back away, his kiss was electric, it felt like a million shock waves had zapped me, like I had been hit by lighting and rumbled by thunder. Such a cold kiss, yet it was warm; his lips were cold but his breath was warm and together it made a foggy lightening that surged through my whole body and left every ounce of me tingling. It was so fierce and yet so gentle, if only I could kiss him forever. His lips were soft, yet the kiss was fierce and passionate and I only realised that I was not dreaming when sirens sounded and blue and red lights flashed through the windows. During this time, we stayed lips locked until he backed away and when he did, I saw his features more clearly. His hair was jet black, like the night he was in, and his face was pale. His features weren't strong but they were thin to the cheekbones and left a fierce impression on anyone who saw them, especially me. He ran away and before I could speak, he was gone and all that was left was the rushing sirens and my thumping heart.

"Rose?" I shouted.

"Chris?" At that time I did not think how I had betrayed Chris, I just yelled.

The sirens seemed to get louder and a voice came from outside, as the door bashed.

"Come out with your hands up!"

How was this wrong, how was any of this wrong? It's my book. I should be able to publish it with my name on the cover. Damn it where are they?

"Chris? Rose?" The door was sealed tight and it trembled under the pressure of whatever the police were using to break it down.

"Over here, quick," Chris called. Thank God, if there is one, thank God you are here Chris. I ran and swooped under the open floorboards Chris held up, as soon as the floorboard slammed onto the ground the door swung open and as we left, we could hear the police's footsteps rattle the ground and the sirens fog the air's silent echoes.

No one saw my name on any of the books, we had been caught on camera and even though we wore our ski masks, they knew it was me, they'd have to be stupid not to know. They didn't name the other two but they named me. For what I did I could have been sent to prison but I don't think I will be, that's about eight books I have published and one has been made into a movie and another into a TV series, both of which I had no control over. As soon as the police found the books and the security tapes, all of the 'written on books' were replaced; they couldn't get rid of them, the book was apparently a big hit.

They searched our rooms, in fact they searched all of the rooms in the school and found nothing, they almost took up the floorboards but Alec objected against it saying that they would have to pay to replace them, which was a cost they didn't want to pay. Throughout the room searches, Chris stayed in the girl's room and refused to split from me.

"Will you make me?" He even said to one of them. He was the acknowledged leader of the group and the so-called rebel. He's not really a rebel; he's just a painted rebel, a fake.

Alec seemed unhappy because Chris was in the girl's room; he would be, of course, anyone would be I suppose, but something didn't seem right, he seemed angry for another reason.

Alec asked to see me in his office and I knew what was coming, the whole school had heard about it. I had tried to get my name published on a book that I did not give in, a bloody good book, and when that failed I had snuck out and written my name on every book in the library, and that was against the law. I knew it would get me in trouble, I just wished that at least one person would know what I had written. The plan didn't succeed anyway, an authority had realised the break-in and had found out what we had done, and then he phoned them and they removed all of the books, all of them. Henry found out all of this; as well as being a wiz with a computer he could find out any news quickly. If only it had followed through, people would have known, maybe things would have changed. They searched our room and found nothing. They were so close to picking up those floorboards, so damn close and it was Alec who saved the day, our hero Alec, as always. We can still go out every Wednesday then; of course, we will have to leave it for a while so that we don't raise suspicion.

The door of Alec's office seemed bigger than usual, it seemed like it would need two hands to open it and maybe a big shove. It seemed to hover and run away from me and for a minute. I could swear that I was running after it and didn't catch it.

Alec opened it and then it was back, normal size but a bigger Alec, he seemed bigger but not angrier.

"Come in," he did not bother to call me by my name or smile. His face was stern, a very fixed stern, it didn't look real, his face seemed like it had been painted on and I had painted it.

"You know why you are here?"

"I do," I said sternly to match his face.

"You don't have to act so sternly with me; I wasn't the one who tried to write my name on the books I made."

"That's because you're not a writer."

"Don't try and get smart with me," he shouted and slammed his hands on the table, he was angry but not because of this. My mind flashed back to when he saw me with Chris and then it hopped back to reality, it couldn't be that, no.

"I'm sorry," I said. "Am I going to be thrown out of the school?"

"No," he said sitting down again. "I have persuaded them to keep you here, you have contributed to many books and I have assured them that this will not happen again. If it does, then, you will have to go."

"I understand," I said, and I did, I wouldn't try it again, not this way anyway. I would get my name out someday though, someday my name would cover those books. Yet, when I looked at Alec, he seemed like he had given up any hope of resisting against *them*, he had given up and this turned my stomach, it turned everything and because of this  I broke down into tears, how could I hold it back anymore, it's just not fair. I should get noticed by those people out there, they should know that it was me who wrote those books, me. Why the hell should my name be hidden, why the hell shouldn't it be shown in golden writing on every cover of every book I have written? Damn them, damn them all to hell and Alec. Alec, why the hell couldn't he see that this is what needs to be done? They need to see my name and every other authors name printed on those books.

"It's not fair," I whimpered, "it's just not fair."

Alec looked at me with his bewildered eyes, they seemed so soft and caring as if he actually wanted to help with my situation, but he couldn't, no one could. He sighed and passed a tissue over the desk, it seemed cold but as his hand touched mine it was warm; in fact, it was steaming hot and sweating. This made me look up into those eyes again and they seemed hungry this time, his eyes dripped with desire, but it couldn't be for me. No it couldn't be for me. Yet he rose from his chair and came around the back of the desk, thinking that when he stood I should stand, I did so and he stopped dead in his tracks. What was wrong with him? He seemed flustered and dizzy, as he began to walk again and he tumbled slightly and took the desk to steady himself, his back was crooked down and as he looked up his breath hardened in the air; I wanted to touch it, I wanted to feel his breath on mine. Carefully, he steadied himself and placed his hand on my shoulder, his other hand wiped away the tears that rapidly streamed down my face. My eyes still quivered with water as he brought me closer to him, he held me there. I was shocked and yet I wanted to hug back; I didn't, I let my arms flop down and I let him embrace me. His body was warm and it made me shiver from how hot it was. Stop this, Alec, I'm with Chris, but then why do I feel heated by your touch? Why do I want to embrace you like you're embracing me? Why do my thighs tingle as if they are excited by your growing pulse? I have to pull away but I don't want to. Slowly, very slowly, I pulled away and did not look up. As I did, so he crooked my chin and made me look at him, he had such beautiful eyes, like Chris' but in blue.

"Don't think about this matter anymore, nothing can be done and I wish it could. I wish to God…"

"If there is one," I reminded.

"I wish every day that you could get your name on those books, you always work so hard, you're so talented," his compliments stung me with a deadly poison that made my cheeks blush. "I would do anything for you, my sweet Emerald Eyes."

Then he embraced me again and this time he sighed with a weighted pleasure as he did so. I did not resist this time and let him unfold me out of his arms in his own time. Such poisonous words he was saying, with such poisonous lips, I wanted to kiss those lips.

I tried to forget about the little hug Alec had given me and then, when I couldn't do that, I pretended it was just a hug between friends. I felt like I had betrayed Chris, I had kissed that anonymous boy at the library and Alec had hugged me. Both were not my own doing but I didn't back away from the kiss, he was the first to edge away and I did not resist as much as I should have when Alec hugged me, especially the second time; I enjoyed them both and to be honest I would do it again, both of them. That boy isn't a big deal, I doubt I will ever see him again and I suppose Alec isn't that much of a big deal either, then again, what if he has feelings for me? No, he can't, but then why am I his Emerald Eyes and no one else's?

I went through day-by-day with my normal routine; tests, stories, greeting Chris. Lately I was a little more forward with Chris because of the whole Alec and mysterious boy in the library thing. I saw that he noticed and rather than asking why, he seemed to take advantage of my early morning kisses and passionate advances. It's not that I particularly wanted to, it's just that I felt obliged to, after all, he was my boyfriend and I didn't feel like breaking up with him any time soon. No, I'm not going to break up with him, no, I won't.

"Hey, Green Eyes," Chris came racing down the hall at full speed, obviously raring to kiss me. He had just finished his tests for the day and so he was completely free, and so was I, oh, joy.

"Hey, Chris," I beamed and he practically swung me around as he grabbed me and kissed both sides of my cheeks. "All done for the day?"

"Yep, and now I get to spend more time with you," oh, more joy. It's not that I didn't like spending time with Chris, I did and sometimes I really did, it's just that lately it seemed more like a chore, as if I was proving to myself that I didn't like Alec in that way and that I didn't like that strange boy either, but I did, I knew I did.

"Guess the rumours have blown over by now, that might be a permanent dot on your record," yeah, it would be. We walked down the hall, his arm wrapped over my shoulder tightly, looking only ahead.

"Yeah, I suppose it will be."


Tuesday greeted a new lesson, introduced recently within the last year. It was KME, Knowledge Machine Education, which introduced the basics about the machines. Why we used them, how they worked, who made them, etc, etc. It wasn't particularly a lesson I looked forward to but since it was run by Alec, I didn't mind it. We would all sit there listening to how the machines worked and wishing they would just make a program that gave us this information. It did give us time to ask questions we wouldn't usually ask though. I watched the room, the windows were long with equally long blinds. It was a small, square of a room with a visual board at the front controlled by touch. I raised my hand.

"Yes, Tanya?"

"Is there any way for information in a person's brain to be taken by the machines?"

"I suppose that is a possibility, however, we would never allow that."

I slumped back into my chair, the lesson was such a drone.

"Now, like I was saying, the way the machines work. Well, when the fibres enter the hole in your neck, they will slither up the spine. This is an unpleasant thought, yes, but at this moment you are unconscious. When they reach the brain, the knowledge will be fed into you by a rather larger fibre using a series of visual and auditory stimulus. The nerve fibres will break and make new connections while this knowledge is being fed into them, and that is how they work. Any more questions?"

A girl from Gold block put up her hand, her name was Louise, also known as Ruby 8.5. "When the machines don't work and they get taken away, where do they go and what happens?"

"Well, usually they'll be tested on a series of machines first, around ten or fifteen. Then they will be taken to the experimenting labs, a calm and safe environment, where the situation will be evaluated and usually they will be sent home for a short period of time."

The lesson ended there. I watched Alec as he walked out, almost drooling a puddle onto the floor.


It took a few weeks but the cloud of rumours passed, well, they weren't rumours. Either way, it had passed and even though it had passed I had been thinking about two things in particular that seemed to bring me back to the subject, Alec and that boy. For a week, Alec didn't teach any classes and he avoided me, I knew he was avoiding me, it was obvious. And that boy, I dreamed about him, I dreamed about him when I should have been dreaming about Chris. He took me away from this place and together we changed the world and then, when everything was right, he held me tight in his arms and leant forward to kiss me, then sirens sounded and the police surrounded us. He still leant in to kiss me and before his lips could touch mine, I woke up, the only thing resembling my dream was my alarm, sounding just as the sirens had done.

Chris and I are continuing as normal, he doesn't know anything about my mixed feelings, that boy or Alec. Even though it has all passed, I feel evil, I feel like a slut, cheating on him.

There was another thing that had stayed on the tip of my mind. The files and how this would affect my record. I don't regret what I did, but if I am to live in this world's future, then I need to know how this will affect it and me. All the records are kept in Alec's office and he keeps his office open because he apparently trusts us.

I snuck away from the Copper block so I could take a look at the records. The door of Alec's room was, as predicted, open and I easily got in.

I shuffled through the desk draws and filing cabinets, I bet there is another room, he doesn't really trust us. As I opened the desk draw and flung papers from side-to-side I noticed a book, a book with 'Shenray' on the title and my name on the cover. It was my book and from where the bookmark was I could tell he had nearly finished it. My book, here, in his desk, here, with my name on it, here. It is illegal to keep these books and yet he kept it, because it was mine, because my name was on it.

"What are you doing in here?" The door slammed shut and Alec scowled at me, then softened his scowl as he saw the book in my hand, my book. He locked the door behind him, I suppose he doesn't want anyone walking in and seeing me and him with a forbidden book, my forbidden book.

"You read my book?" My heart suddenly started pounding and I didn't expect it to, having this forbidden book in my hand, my forbidden book. This was all forbidden, even locking the door while having a student in his office was forbidden, he was breaking the rules, for me, to read my book.

His gaze swiftly fell to the floor and he seemed like a school boy scolded, no, not scolded, smitten. "I've read all of your books."

"But this book…"

"Is forbidden," Alec started. He edged closer to the desk and I came out from behind it with the book still in my hand, shaking. "But it's the only book with your name on and I couldn't not read a book made by my favourite author. I have all of her books." All of my books, there were plenty of other people in this school who had made books, and most were much better than me, Amber Chasley has had five books made into movies, way more than me. I was his favourite author, he had all my books.

"You have all my books?"

"I'm surprised you haven't noticed, they're all up there on the shelf," and they were, they were all there, every single one without another book in their presence.

"Do you like it?" I asked.

"It's one of your best." That didn't answer my question. "I love it," that did, "I love… all your books." For a minute in that pause I thought he was going to say something else, besides he loves all my books.

"Which bit do you like best?"

He edged closer, closer, closer until he was little than an inch away from me, then he stopped.

"My favourite bit," he considered, leaning forward so that I could hear his gentle whispers. I blushed, my heart was near to bursting and it was obvious that I was heated by how close he was.

"My favourite bit," he repeated, his breath now resting on my cheek, "was when Shenray finally found the girl he was looking for and realised that he couldn't be with her, and so he took her in his arms," and as he said this he did the same and wrapped his arms around my waist, there was nothing between us now, "then he slowly edged closer," and he did the same, "and gave her the last kiss he would ever be able to give her." My eyes were closed and my lips were parted and as Alec was an inch away, I could feel his hot breath circling my lips and then, as if realising that what he was doing was something for a dream, he let go and backed away.

"You should go," he took the book from my hand, brushing against me as he did so; it made us both shiver, but not a cold shiver, a warm embracing shiver.

"I…" speechless, I was speechless, why did you stop, my dear Shenray.

"Why are you here Emeral… Tanya?"

"Emerald Eyes," I corrected, it was much better than my name now, it was his name for me, for me.

"Why were you here?"

I told him everything, "I wanted to find the files, I know they're kept about every student and I wanted to see the damage I had caused."

"How do you know about the files?" Henry, but I wasn't going to tell him that.

"I just do."

He considered this for a while then thought it unnecessary to ask any further questions, "The damage is pretty bad but if you keep writing books like they want, then you'll be fine. Is the book for your next deadline almost done?"

"Deadline, what deadline? I already had a book published this week."

"That book doesn't count as it was published illegally, I'm sorry, Emerald 2.0."

I was furious, any passion I had felt was gone, this wasn't fair and why was he calling me that name? I was his Emerald Eyes, not 2.0. Why is he trying to distance us, and then I realised, if he didn't try to distance us he would do something that wasn't allowed.

I started a new subject, "Did you like the bit where Zeta went to find Shenray?" That was the bit where they ended up sleeping together and I described that scene in great detail, it was a passionate scene.

"It was one of my favourite scenes," I could see his mind flash back to the images he got when reading that scene, his face became

44

dazed and confused and suddenly I saw a flash of red cross him, but not a flash of anger, a flash of lust, he wanted me and though I would admit it to no one, I wanted him too.

His hand stroked my cheek and suddenly the rush of hot that surrounded my body rubbed off onto him and he encased both his hands on my cheeks, my Shenray, you are my Shenray, Alec. His lips were hot and rough. This was not a boy's kiss, this was a man's kiss and it caressed my slipping tongue and my blooming lips until all I could feel was the hotness of his touch and the caress of his gentle hands. They slipped to my waist and pulled me to the couch so that I was placed beside the right side of the door. He lay on top of me, fully clothed and fully hot; I swear I could undress him now and feel him press against me, but Chris. Though his touch got warmer and his hand slipped to my breast, I could think of nothing but Chris and then that boy. Why, why are these thoughts in my head? I don't love you, Chris, I can never love you, but I don't love you either, Alec, what am I doing? He was so warm, so inviting, I wanted him to hold me, but Chris. I had to pull away and so I did, it hurt when I did and I flinched as if our hearts had already been stitched together and we had already formed one.

Alec looked at me with his lust-filled eyes, those blank blue eyes, they sighed for my kiss. His face was shocked, as if it was a dream, a dream that he should have stayed in and now it was a nightmare because it should not have happened, it should have stayed in his dreams, like that boy stayed in mine.

"I'm sorry," Alec almost looked close to tears and I suppose I did too, I was just shocked. *I am so shocked.*

"No, it's ok, I…" what was I going to say? 'I loved it,' 'I love you,' because I did love it but I don't love him.

"You should go," Alec opened the door, then straightened himself out, something he should have done before opening the door.

"I…" his voice echoed in my ear, for a moment, just a moment there was just me and him.

"Yeah," I smiled, my hand reaching to touch his face, it was gentle with the occasional stubble and as I placed my hand on his cheek, he was warm and he closed his eyes. I only took away my hand when I heard footsteps rumble the corridor floor, it was Chris.

"Green Eyes," he beamed, they had obviously liked his latest painting, he pulled me by the waist and hugged me from behind.

Alec was shocked at first and then he snapped into reality and laughed, "Look after her."

"I always do," Chris smiled and placed his head on my shoulder, "Green Eyes, you're all warm." I was still warm from Alec's kiss.

"Must be the air conditioning, I'll check it out. I'm a bit warm myself, actually." Alec walked away before anything else was said, before he could snatch me away from Chris and hold me like he wanted to.

"They… liked your picture then?" I looked into Chris's eyes, where had the blue gone? No Chris's eyes are hazel not blue, or a powdered ash-mauve, they're hazel.


Another book, it's ridiculous, I already made a damn good book. This new one was coming along quickly and it seemed that I would have a lot of spare time; it was about a girl stuck between two men, a rebel and an authority. The book resembled me and I had no doubt that when Alec would read it, that he would know this, Chris won't read it and even if he did he wouldn't understand, he wouldn't know. That's partly because he's not in it, he is neither the rebel nor the authority, Alec is the authority and that boy, he is the rebel. Because no one else knows about that boy or has seen him I am free to use his looks, his facial features that leave an impression, his jet black hair and his ash-mauve eyes, and yet I didn't use him in this book, it almost seemed wrong to do so. The rebel in the book symbolised him but it was nothing like him at all, not that I could judge on what he was like.

If only I could see him again, just for a second, I'd be tempted to slap him in a way for just kissing me, but I'd also be tempted to

46

kiss him again. It seemed so much like a dream, boys don't just go round sneaking into libraries and kissing girls, I'm sure they don't.

"Tanya?" Luke waved a hand in front of my face, damn artists think they can wake me up from my trance. Luke was said to be equal to Chris in art but none would ever say that, especially not Luke, he had brown eyes and brown hair, all in all he was rather plain, in my opinion.

"We have to go, it's lesson time, Dudet."

"Huh, lesson time, hardly lessons."

"Either way," Luke shrugged, "Come on, everyone else is already there."

"Then why aren't we?"

"Because you're wrapped up in your new book and I was wrapped up in my new painting." I looked at his painting, it was extraordinary like all his others, it wasn't finished yet so making it out was hard, but it was still extraordinary, half finished anyway, it was better than any of Chris's, though Chris didn't really like me looking at his work; Luke liked to show off.

"Come on, Tanya 2.0," he liked to do that a lot, mainly because it annoyed people. Overall, he was quite an irritating person, you needed one in every group, it means when you have nothing to talk about you can talk about how annoying the annoyer is.

Lessons, they weren't lessons they were like leeches reversed, sucking blood into you instead. Chris, Rose, Sophie, Jasper, Luke, Lucy and I all attached to these chairs in a row. I would always look at Chris as they attached the equipment to the back of my neck. Everyone had a hole where the wire was placed at the back of the neck, it was a permanent mark and it was very high up and hardly visible. Anyone who didn't have a mark in the outside world was seen as a freak; I think it's the other way around, just once I'd like to see a person without a mark on their neck. I looked at Chris because I was always afraid, afraid in case it didn't work this time and they took me for experiments, afraid in case they did the same to anyone else in this room, afraid because while it happened, we were unconscious and unaware of the world surrounding us. The metal neck brace was placed around my neck and the wire attached into my neck, it was like being sent to death and having the noose placed around you, a cold, metal noose. All the wires fixed up to one machine, they used to be separate machines for everyone, but now they have advanced even more in technology. There, on the machine, is a touch-type screen that they will operate and feed us the basic knowledge we need to know, that is according to them. I can feel it tingling my neck, when it first starts it hurts and you will hear a little gasp of air or a yelp come from everyone around you; they say you get used to it, lies, all lies. It always hurts and some say it hurts even more with the more knowledge you get given. The shock started pushing and pulling through my body and then my head dropped, I wasn't looking at Chris this time, but I knew he was looking at me and expected me to look back.

I don't know what everyone else feels when they are in that state, where the machines are controlling you and feeding you knowledge. I feel strange, I feel as if I am in a dream that is real; first I am always falling but I can't see where, I can feel myself touching something and then strings of light will surround me, I reach out to touch them but when I do, they dissolve and disperse in the air. This time it was slightly different, I swear I could hear Alec's voice and I could feel his hot hand touch my cheek, only it wasn't, it can't have been. When I woke from the machines, Alec was in the room staring at me from the other side, had he touched me? Had he spoke to me, please say yes, my sweet Shenray, my demanding authority.

"Are you ok, Green Eyes?"

"Yeah, I'm fine, I just need to talk to Alec about my book. I'm a bit worried about it."

"Ok then, cinema tonight?"

"Yeah."

"I'll see you in fifteen for the tests."

"Ok." One worded answers seemed to be going round a lot lately.

Alec had gone back to his office; I knocked and entered without hearing a reply. He rose from his seat and dropped the pen onto his desk, he seemed almost scared of me, almost.

"Alec did you talk to me when I was hooked to the machine, did you touch me?"

His guilty eyes said it all, why was he doing this, why did he feel like this? He could have anyone, talented, handsome, why did he like me?

"Yes, I brushed your cheek." Lie, he held his hand on my cheek for longer.

"Do you like me, Alec?" How could he deny it?

"Yes," truth. "Ever since the day you came here I knew you were special, different, you are my Emerald Eyes." I was his Emerald Eyes; he thought I was special, different.

"Why?"

"I don't know. I just know that ever since the day you came here I began to feel things for you, I don't know why." I didn't want that answer, it wasn't an answer, it was nothing.

He came round from his desk and pulled me close to him like he had done that day, when his breath was so hot and his body was so hot, he stroked away my hair and whispered into my ear, "I love you." But I don't love you.

The door wasn't locked and when Chris came in, I didn't resist from Alec's grip, the scene froze and all that was seen was Alec and me and the blank stare of Chris, his hazel stolen from his gaze. Alec let go and Chris said nothing against what had happened.

"Tests are starting soon, let's go," he whispered, "Tanya." I could almost feel the glare he focused on Alec and then, as I walked in front of him, the glare that he threw at me. He said nothing and that was worse than anything. We both walked to the testing rooms in silence and took the test in front of us. We could leave when it was done.

The test were handed out, we could start as soon as we got it, the usual rules applied, name, date, signature, and at the end we have to fill out the subject area we believed it to be. It was large but easily done in less than an hour. After it was done, I looked towards Chris. At first, I did not look at his anxious face or trembling hands, I just felt like I had betrayed him, my stomach turned inside out, *he must hate me*. He seemed nervous, *I hope to God, if there is one, that I have not affected this test for him, otherwise what might happen.*

As Chris was 'the leader', we waited for him and we waited for a long time, something was wrong.

"He's taking his time," Luke said.

"Do you think?" Lucy looked towards me.

"No, he'll be fine," I assured her, and as soon as I said that, he came out and a great sigh blew over us.

"You alright, Chris?" Jasper smiled. "Took your time."

"Yeah, I just had some things on my mind," I did not dare to look and see him staring at me, making the rest of the group look as well.


When we were alone, Chris brought up the conversation as expected, "Do you like him then, how long has it been going on for?"

"Chris, nothing has happened, I swear," lie.

"Then why?"

"I don't know, he just hugged me, I was shocked, I didn't know what to do, I didn't like it." Lie.

"Please, Chris, you have to believe me." Why should he? "Nothing has happened and nothing ever will, I love you." The biggest lie I have ever told and it worked, he had never heard those words pass my lips before and he demanded to hear it again.

"What?"

"I said, I love you." Why was I lying? "Please believe me, I love you." I cried, perhaps I could be an actor instead of a writer; I was obviously very good at it.

"Just be careful round him," he hugged me, so naive, so trusting, Chris don't, "I love you too." But I don't love you, Chris; I will never love you, never.

We went to the cinema that night and Chris was very clingy, he kept me close to him, he held my waist, he held my hand, he kept his arm around my shoulder, even throughout the whole movie as if Alec was watching us. He advanced on me a lot and if I had refused he would know what I said was a lie, it was all lies, he tried to kiss me hard, to caress me softly as if he was trying to be the man that he was not and Alec was; you will never be a man, Chris, you will always be a boy, you will live as a boy and you will die as a boy.

# Chapter 3

I don't know who the news hit harder, us or Chris. His test came back wrong, it was all wrong and when they checked the machine it was working perfectly. He's been taken to be tested on a selection of machines, one hundred machines, it would kill him, it would take a week at least and if ten come back negative he will be taken forever. No one who has been taken has come back and every time a random selection of machines is chosen for them to use, ten or more are always negative, he stands no chance. Chaos was at an outbreak in the Copper block, no one could work without Chris, no one could do anything, we were afraid and in a way I felt as if this was my own doing, as if the scene with Alec and me had made him fail, it was my fault. I don't love him but I can't live without him. We just had to wait for the news; we would know in a week, a week without Chris, a week without him, what would we all do.

We waited a week and still Chris did not come back; we knew that he would never come back when a new person arrived, she was quiet and shy. No one cared; we all hated her because with her here, it meant Chris would never come back. She was thin and slight with pale hair to match her pale skin and blue eyes, a demon in an angel's body. No one tried to make friends with her and so she often went out and met with other people from the Tin block, and anything lower than copper.

"We have to get him back," Henry slammed a book down on the table, it was night time and we had called a meeting, the other girl was out with friends.

"They took his paintings today." I was so confused, they had come so quickly, I just wish I had taken one to remember him by, just one.

"What?" Lucy said.

"Yeah, they came and took any paintings in his room and on his wall." I looked out of the window as if doing this would make Chris appear, it didn't, he isn't appearing.

"What do we do?" Rose sighed and that sigh was followed by many others. What could we do? There was no hope now.

Later on in the night, when everyone was trying to sleep, trying but never succeeding as the thought of Chris was on their mind, Henry came into the girl's room.

"Tanya," I didn't need waking up, I wasn't asleep. "Come with me."

We went out into the hall and sat side-by-side to talk, "I know where they've taken him."

"How?"

"How do I know all my information, I just do," he snapped. "It's not far from here, if you were to take the passage then there would be an alley on Thirty-Four Street, down the alley is a door with graffiti on it that says, 'Davis was 'ere,' pull that out and it will take you to Thirty-Eight Street, from there you go down the alley and into the street where there is a grid, go into it and then follow the direction of the water. Pass the first two ladders then, when you get to the last, it will look differently made, go up that one and you will be there and it should be close to the experimenting rooms. I know you won't be able to get him back but at least you can talk to him."

"What about you?"

"Only one of us can go. Alec will suspect if more aren't to be seen, he counts, you know. Besides, you have no lessons tomorrow and you…"

"Don't say it, just leave it, I'll get my things. Thank you, Henry."

"No one else knows, if they did they would want to go. Be careful, Tanya, be safe."

"I will."

"Wait, take this," he handed me a device that was like one of those torches you put on your head. It was thin and cold to the tough.

"What is it?"

"Just wear it on your head. Any camera won't detect you if you wear it."

"Thank you," Henry nodded.

Down the passage, go to Thirty-Four Street, the door with 'Davis was 'ere', to Thirty-Eight Street, into the street and down the grate, follow the water and pass the first three ladders, no two, stop at the third. It's different from the others and go up it, then I'm in. It shouldn't take me that long and if it goes on till tomorrow then its ok, I have no classes; I must find Chris and tell him the truth.

The place was big and I searched for hours on end for Chris, the whole place was a pure white maze with rooms dotted about crisscrossing corners. I marked my location with a marker pen, a small dot that no one but me would notice. When I heard footsteps I would have to hide wherever I could, in cupboards, under beds, behind doors. I searched for so long, hours on end and as my heart raced in the first few minutes it slowed down as I continued to search. I was hungry, thirsty, tired but I had to find Chris, I had to tell him the truth.

I contemplated resting, after all there were beds, and the place was clean, too clean, but I couldn't let anyone find me so I continued with my exhaustion weighing me down. I felt as if it wasn't only my lack of food, or restless nights that was causing my exhaustion, as I following the constant, white corridors, the place I had been told was friendly and comforting just seemed fake. The walls were too bright and the rooms were bare except for the beds, now and then there were rooms with equipment in, but I saw hardly any people. This made me optimistic; I thought perhaps they didn't experiment on many people. But I knew I was lying to myself, the air looked pure, but felt thick and it felt as if the walls should be stained.

Four hours, it took me four hours to find him and when I did it wasn't what I had expected. He wasn't in a white room with a bed like all the other rooms I had seen throughout this maze. The room was small, with what seemed like metal lockers up and down the wall, they had numbers engraved on them, 20 to 30, two sets of five across the wall facing the door. The door had a code on it, but it was open, as if I was being invited in. Chris was behind a screen, I could see the back of his head and yet when I called he did not turn and answer me. No one else was in the room and when I closed the door, I called out to him again.

"Chris, it's me, Tanya." No reply. "Please don't be mad, please turn around."

"I can't." Finally an answer but why couldn't he turn around.

"I'll come around."

"Don't!"

Silence. "Chris, why?"

"Just leave this place Green Eyes." Green Eyes, good he wasn't mad at me then.

"Chris, whatever it is, I can handle it."

"Promise me you won't be scared?"

"Chris?"

"Promise!"

"Ok, I promise."

As I walked to the screen I could see Chris's face more clearly, it was sad. When I came around the screen I wanted to shout, yell, scream but I had promised that I would not be scared, I had promised that I would be brave. Chris's head was still the same, but his body wasn't, it was gone. His whole body had been taken away from his head, all that was left was the vertebrae coming out from the neck and down, it was attached to a translucent screen that also had his nerves spreading from the spine to each side. Now and then, the board would flash small circles of light here and there, sometimes red and sometimes green. I promised I wouldn't scream, but Chris stood there; no, he wasn't standing, he was there with no body attached to a board with his spine and his nerves spread out. What are they doing to him? Why would they do this? They are monsters, cruel, vile, inhumane monsters, all of them.

"Where is…" 'Your body' say it damn it, say it!. 'Chris, where is your body.'

"In that drawer over there, it's hooked up to wires," I could see his mouth move and his eyes turn to the drawer. How was this possible? He shouldn't be alive, it's not possible. How is he talking, how?

I went to what I thought was a locker and opened it, it was long and showed Chris's naked body covered with wires and fixed to a machine. I don't know what scared me more, his headless body or his bodiless head.

"Leave, Tanya, you can't do anything." He was right, what could I do? "They have me fed up to energy so my brain is nourished, but without my body it won't last very long. They are monsters, Tanya, criminals; they tear people apart and use their bodies and minds. The brain is what they want; they tear every lobe apart and every nerve. They kill people for their work. All those people who have come here because of failing those tests are dead, I will die." *Don't say it.* "They will experiment on me until I die so that they can unravel the mysteries of the human mind and the world, they're insane."

"I'll find a way to get you out of here, somehow…"

"No, I want you to leave now and never ever come back here; if they find you, they will do the same to you or worse. Leave and never come back, just run, please, Tanya, run." Then something sounded, it wasn't an alarm or a siren, it was a trigger, it beeped three times then shocked, it shocked Chris and I almost cried as he winced and shrieked with pain. His colour was fading; his face was so pale now, so drained. His eyes had lost their blue touch, no hazel; they had lost their hazel touch. I wanted to tell him the truth, but how could I? What person would tell another that they didn't love him while he was like this? 'Chris I don't love you,' I doubt those words will ever pass my tongue.

"Go!" He shrieked and I did, I ran away the way I had come, I never wanted to see it again, not any of it, never again.


Alec was in his office again, he didn't come out much these days. It was partly his fault, I'm sure he could have stopped it; he could have stopped them from taking away Chris.

"Alec," he turned around and for once, I did not notice the gleam in his twinkling eye, or his rugged looks, I noticed everything else. The shelves that neatly sat on both sides of the desk, the two sofas that sat on each side of the door, the room was almost symmetrical. I noticed the desk and it's small, green-copper phone as well as the paper and stationary scattered about, but I didn't notice him, I didn't want to.

"Emerald Eyes, I haven't seen you in a while."

"Get him back, Alec, I know you can."

His silence told me everything, 'I don't want him back'. "It's not that simple."

"Yes, it is," I snapped, "all you have to do is phone, make up an excuse, think on the spot."

"You're putting me on the spot."

"Don't try and change the subject, Sir, just get him back and if you don't, I swear I will tell the whole world what you did," he looked at me hesitantly as if this was a new me he would have to adjust to, his smile told me that he would adjust to whatever I became; whatever I do, he will always love me. He took the small phone in his hand and a screen materialised just above it. He presses the private call option, that way a video chat wouldn't be setup, then dialled. I listened to every word and he was aware of this.

"You have a pupil of mine who failed ten machines. Correct, Chris Williams, Chrysocolla 3.8."

The voice from the phone was muffled and husky, "That is correct."

"I need him back, a pupil has found out what happens to them and is threatening."

"Who?"

"It doesn't matter who, it just matters that they know."

"We can sort them out, take them away," my eyes widened and I suddenly imagined myself next to Chris with my body gone and my nerves spread out on a clear board for all eyes to see.

"No, other people already know but if he comes back, things will be sorted out, they will be kept quiet and later on, they can be turned to the association, that way no leaks will spill."

"He's not in a fit state to come back."

"I don't care, whatever you've done to him just put it back. If his legs are gone, give him new ones, no one will notice, just get him back or something that cannot be controlled will happen." He slammed the phone down on the table and sighed, placing his fingers spread out on his forehead.

"Happy?" he asked. I walked away and did not reply.

"Emerald Eyes." Don't call me that. "Wait." I kept walking and he went in front of the door to stop me from exiting my scene.

"Have I upset you?" Yes, yes you have, you could have stopped this all along. You're just like them. You know what happens there and you let it go on, you let them take Chris, you're just like them, a monster.

He touched my cheek and I flung it off, filthy demon, then he forced his hands to my face and gave me a hard kiss. His lips were truly poison and I did not want it corrupting me, I struggled to get loose but his grip was fierce and he held me by the waist. Get off, Alec. I slapped him and he gripped my hand and brought it close to his chest.

"Do you not love me anymore?" I never loved you, I never said I loved you, I don't love anyone. "Will you be mine when he comes back, not his?" No, never, I am no ones, I hate you.

"Let me leave now," by telling him to phone I was keeping the secret of what he did to me, if they found out he had even touched me it would be his head separated from his body. If I told, Chris would go back to that hell.

Chris came back and that nobody left. Thank God, if there is one, that he's back. The first thing he did was hug me, he knew it was me, he knew I had saved him and I was glad that he didn't ask why.

When night came and everyone had celebrated Chris's triumphant return after many 'What happened?' and 'what was it like?' Scary, it was scary, I could answer all of those questions for him, some he did not know himself, but I did. He told me to come to his room, everyone else had gone out.

"How did you do it?" he asked. I can't tell you, Chris.

"Can we just focus on you being back?" He was undressing, going to sleep, it wasn't that late, only nine o'clock.

"Did you have to do something with him?"

"No," I said disgusted with the words and the images in my head, "I told him to get you back or I would tell…"

"Tell what?" he turned from me to take off his t-shirt.

"I would tell them that he kissed me." The truth would come out sooner or later and I could tell that the truth hurt as Chris winced. "I didn't kiss him, Chris."

"Did he hurt you?" What would you do even if he did? As I watched him take of his shirt I saw the scar that surrounded his spine; there were stitches and in some areas the wound was still open and the skin had not stretched back over the vertebrae. They had obviously done a very poor job of it and didn't care about the outcome, it was a rush job.

"No, he didn't hurt me," I walked closer to him and placed my hand on the top of his spine. "And what about you, does it hurt?" *Yes, of course it hurts, how could something that looks so painful not hurt?* I stroked down the spine and he curved to my touch.

"I'm fine," how brave, "I'm just glad I'm out of there. I imagine that if there is a hell it would be like that. I saw so many other things, they would cut people apart and attach them together with other people's body parts, they would take out the brain leaving men and women for dead so that they could fiddle with it, play with it. They carved up bones and chopped up human flesh as if it was an animal's meat ready to be cooked. They used bones in circuits and melted flesh to see how their new inventions would work; we were rats, no, we were worse than any rat, we were human sacrifices, human experiments starved and drained of energy, prodded and poked until we were dead. Hell, that is hell and for that reason, I don't want to die, for that reason I want to find an eternity where it is just me, me and you." I don't, sometimes I want death to rid me off this place, I'm already in hell, and an eternity with you, Chris would still not make me love you, I can never love you, Chris.

He still faced the wall as I wrapped my arms around him; whether or not I loved him, he had still been in an ordeal and the truth would kill him and drag him down to that pit that was hell.


Things had been going around school, not about Chris, just things in general. Alec tried to dismiss any talk as nonsense about the experimenting labs being evil and cold places, but we all knew it wasn't nonsense. We had been talking about rebelling, taking down the school, the whole world. Unfortunately, we knew it was all just a pipe dream and nothing would ever really change.

"We have to rebel, we have to do something," Henry said. He had become somewhat of a rebel these days and it was respected in our little group.

"What can we do?" Rose already knew the answer, 'nothing', there was nothing we could do, they were all following a dream that would lead to a nightmare, it will never happen, this world will never be as it was in those lost days of forgotten memories; I wish someone could remember, I wish they could tell me, tell all of us, everyone.

"We can't do anything?"

"Green Eyes."

"Well, really, Chris what do you expect us to do, we've tried to rebel, it doesn't work, we get caught. I got caught."

"We have to tell people what happens."

"So what," I snapped, "we just become some sort of rebel group, we go around telling the world what they do, what they're really like. It won't happen."

"What if…" Sophie started.

"Yes," a now scolded Chris said.

"We graffiti."

"Graffiti? What will that do?" Jasper said.

"Just think about it, we graffiti everywhere, we write a message, something strong that will get people to think, everywhere, every Wednesday."

"That's ridiculous, every wall is fitted with an anti-graffiti solution now. It won't work." They weren't listening to my attempts to stop them.

"Please," Henry laughed, "as if there isn't a way around that."

"What would the message be?" Lucy was excited; she liked these sorts of crazy ideas, "How many people, and every Wednesday?"

"Same as always, five every Wednesday, and the message needs to be something poetic, something that will get people to think."

I knew all eyes were on me, with two artists in the group, two sports players, two dancers, a musician and a singer and an actor in the group, I was the only writer, meaning I was the one to think of the poetic but thinking message.

"No," I flipped onto my bed and turned away from them, "Do it yourself."

"Green Eyes?"

"Chris, leave it." No one refused Chris. "I'm not."

Ruby placed a hand on my shoulder and rolled me over, "Please, Tanya."

"Fine," I sighed, "but I want nothing to do with this, I just write the message."

"So you won't come tomorrow?" Lucy said.

"No, I'll give you the message tomorrow." A message, a message, but what message?


'Feeding knowledge, killing cells, deadly machines of useless murderers.' It would have to do, they wouldn't wait, they wanted to go tonight. It wasn't that bad, but I'm sure with more time I could have thought of something better.

"Do you have the message?" Chris said, he had been in a foul mood lately, mainly with me.

"Yeah," everyone scurried around to listen but I just threw the piece of paper in their direction and let them read it. "It would have been better but you didn't give me that much time."

"No, it's perfect." Sophie, the new master mind of plans.

"It's your Wednesday night you know; we've got the spray cans ready. Henry made them." Chris was annoying me so much lately and I couldn't figure out why.

"Yeah, I know. What colour is the spray paint?"

"Red, it makes a statement." Henry said, finally getting an input on the plan. "Last chance, Tanya, it's either you coming or Jasper."

"Who else is coming?"

"Henry, Sophie, Lucy, Malic and you if you want," Chris answered.

"What about you?"

"I'm going next week." Thank God, if there is one, then I'll go. I just want to be away from him, he is so irritating, his face just leaks depression as if he is constantly searching for sympathy, it's pathetic. If I go tonight, it means I don't have to see him every Wednesday night, perfect.

"Fine, I'll come, pass us a spray can." And then we were gone, down the passage and away from the school again, dressed in black with covering masks and away from Chris, finally away from him.

We sprayed the message on shop windows, covered security cameras with red, sprayed it on every street corner, down every nook and cranny that could be seen and couldn't. We sprayed it on walls and libraries, everywhere and I loved it. I loved the joy of feeling rebellious, the anxiousness of not wanting to be caught, it was exhilarating and as adrenaline filled my whole body with a thirst for truth, my writing became fiercer; I was on edge, the edge of the world, the edge of life and I wanted to stay there, forever.

Down one alleyway I swear I saw someone, but not just any someone, it was him, that boy with those mesmerising eyes, those sweet, powdered ash-mauve eyes. He was standing there watching me as I spray painted the message onto the wall and I wanted to show him it was me, I wanted to take off my mask and touch him, and just look into those eyes, those sweet, powdered ash-mauve eyes. *I'm dreaming, he can't be there, here.* The spray can dropped from my hand as I saw him and he caught it and finished writing what I had started. I had already written 'Feeding knowledge, killing cells, deadly...' and he finished it, differently and it now read, 'Feeding knowledge, killing cells, deadly sins the likes of hell.' My mouth wouldn't move, why can't I speak, I just stood there looking into those eyes through my woolly mask. He handed me the spray can and then I swear we were back in the library because the same sirens sounded and the same blue and red lights flickered. Only this time it was louder and the lights were brighter, this boy seemed to attract the authorities wherever he was; the library, here and now... *he's gone.* The police were still here though and I began to panic, we had been through what we would do if this happened, go straight to the passageway and don't look for anyone. I ran, catching hope on my fading breaths I ran and did not look back to see if I was being pursued; I only stopped when the passage was in sight and the echoing sirens and flashing lights had become nothing but a blur in sound and in sight.

"Is everyone here?"

"Yes," Henry nodded.

"Thank God."

"If there is one," he corrected.

"What was it like?" Ruby asked.

"Crazy, the police showed up."

"Really?"

"Don't exaggerate, Tanya," Henry protested.

"I'm not, they did turn up."

"I was on the same street as you, Thirty-Eight Street, there were no police."

I remembered the scene at Thirty-Eight Street and the flashing lights and sirens, I can't have imagined it, they were there on Thirty-Eight Street. All streets were renamed as numbers in the capital, everywhere else had place names; I don't know why they did this, just another form of control.

"You must have left before me."

"No, I didn't and I saw that new thing you sprayed, how did you come up with that?"

"With what?"

"Feeding knowledge, killing cells, deadly sins the likes of hell," he said. I didn't write that, it was him, him, and he was there, I swear he was there, and I swear the police were there too and sirens. I know I heard sirens.

"It just came to me."

"Well it's good; we'll use that as well."

We were on the news, our message was on the news. Just think how many people saw it. This could actually work, it could actually make a difference and I helped, it was my message on those walls, mine and all... and his, his was there too. They had caught us on camera but we were wearing masks so our faces aren't identifiable. We were careful not to touch anything and leave fingerprints; knowledge isn't the only technology that's advanced these days, mobiles, surveillance equipment. Everything's changed.

"We are unaware who these law breakers are, but we are assured that what they have written is false and goes against all policies and laws." Ha, false, what were they talking about?

"Turn it up," Ruby shouted.

"We suspect that these crimes may have been committed by a group of criminals that are on the loose, known as 'knowledge rejecters'. The knowledge we are given is given to us with trust and care, we are very lucky to have it. If you see these people, please report them to the authorities immediately."

The faces came up on the screen, a few people who I didn't know, no big deal. They weren't us so it didn't matter, until his face showed up. Why is he there? So, he's a criminal; no, they're not criminals, that's a lie, they're just like us, rebels. He's a rebel, he's a real rebel.


We continued to sneak out every Wednesday for a month and the media got more and more interested in us. I didn't see the boy again, only in my dreams, the same dream where he took me away and I'd always wake up before his lips met mine. After two rounds of spray painting we also printed off posters with a rhyme on, made by me;

Slaughter, murder,
That's our job
Hunt and kill
A murdering mob
Knowledge, knowledge fills your brains
Swell up; swell up, drip red to drains

They will take you
They will come
When you can't learn
And it takes just one.

Genius, they can't stop it, people have seen so many already. The media try to cover it, saying it's wrong and saying that what happens is right. But people are beginning to think for themselves and the knowledge they've been given is going against the knowledge itself. Ha, that'll show them. Just wait, things will change, people will question, the world will change because of the ten of us and then, when it does, I will publish my books and have my name on cover after cover, my dream will be seen, it will.

# Chapter 4

Even though our rebellions have changed the way a few people think, it doesn't mean that everything has changed. We are still hooked up to machines like animals, like test subjects. Chris was dismissed from going on them for a while but he'd always watch, especially when Alec was around watching too, mostly watching me. He would wait outside the tests rooms for everyone as well; God, if there is one, he's annoying.

The test was on what I determined to be biology, as usual I yawned and flicked open the page knowing the test would, like always, be a breeze. Yet, when I read the question, I had to read it again, and again, and again. I didn't know, the questions were in front of me but the answers that usually unfolded in front of my eyes were not. Why, why me, anyone else but me, please not me.

"No," Henry swivelled around to see me dripping sweat onto the paper; I wish I could be like him, even if he wasn't given the knowledge he would be fine. He reads so many books, he's naturally smart. Henry, help.

"Exam conditions," came a shout.

No, I'm just worried, I can do this. 'The three stages of ultra filtration in the kidneys,' I don't know. 'The role of ADH?' What's ADH? Why, why can't I do this? What went wrong?

I was told to go to the lesson rooms and there they told me that my test was wrong, all wrong. No, God, no, please let there be a god and please let him save me from this, this hell, the hell I will surely go to. I was put on the same machine and then I took the test, negative. Then I was placed on another and another and another, again and again and again. I had already been tried on 97 machines and with every machine, it felt like I was being drained more and more each time. I had come back negative on nine already, just let me get through these. It seemed I was failing all the basics; the English level 6 programme, Maths level 8, Biology level 8, Chemistry level 8, Physics level 8, French level 9, Spanish level 7, English level 7, Maths level 9, just one more to go.

I was hooked up to the machine and it was the last time I would ever feel this cold steel press against my neck, I was sure of it. Level 9 Biology, it sucked away my essence, my everything; I wanted to stay, I wanted to live and see the world change, please let me stay. Alec watched the whole time, the monster, the vicious monster, scum. The test was negative, I knew as soon as I looked at the cover, the only cover that ever has my name on it, test papers that I had failed. They sat me down and Alec was there to, scum. Then I saw it all, this was the end of my life. I would be placed in hell like Chris was; Alec had already gotten out one student, he couldn't do it again. I would die, cut up into pieces, with every nerve fibre taken from my brain and examined like gold; I didn't want to die, not like this, not now.

"Wait a minute," Alec said. "You've used the same test twice."

"What?" A man snatched the paper from his hand and examined the paper as closely as he would examine my brain, "Level 8 Biology, I swear we did different ones, the machine will know." He pressed the touch screen and pressed it hard, scrolling down and finding that Alec was right, but was he? I swear I had done ten different tests; English level 6 programme, Maths level 8, Biology level 8, Chemistry level 8, Physics level 8, French level 9, Spanish level 7, English level 7, Maths level 9 and Biology level 9.

"You're right," the man said. It's here, two tests twice. One more test to replace it then, how about level 9 biology then?"

"It's similar to level 8; the girl will know the answers because of it. Try something new, something like English level 8."

Level 8, I'm sure that's sentence structures and paragraphing, there's no way I'll fail that, even if I don't know it, I am a writer after all.

"Very well," and there it was again that twinge and tweak I thought I wouldn't feel again, I had never been glad to feel it.

The test came back positive, I was safe.

We continued our rebellions and still they had no clue it was us; perfect, absolutely perfect. We continued for another month, people where thinking now, I'm sure they were.

Alec asked to see me in his office again, damn him. I hope he dies. I hate him.

"Will you be ok?"

"I'll keep the door wide open, Chris." I remember when I came back from testing Chris hugged me and refused to let go. I needed that hug, but not from him.

I did keep the door wide open, even when Alec told me to shut it; he would have no cooperation from me.

"What do you want?"

"I want," he sniped, "you to stop these rebellions, let it rest, Tanya."

"What rebellions?" He'd get nothing from me.

"Don't even try to lie. If you don't stop, I swear I'll make you take that level 9 biology programme and test and cut you up myself."

It was him, he had saved me, he had swapped it, I knew he had, but why?

"I love you, Tanya," liar, "but when you do things like this, it can get out of hand, they're finding a lead, they'll know, stop it, now."

"I don't know what you're talking about, sir. Now if you'll excuse me, I have a book to write."

"I'll make you stop, Tanya; I'll make you all stop."

Ha, you won't stop us, they'll know, the whole world will know, "Just try and stop me!"

It was another Wednesday night and it was our turn to stay in and cover if the pratfects came round. Chris stayed this Wednesday, complaining that he never got to see me on Wednesday nights anymore. I wish he had gone with them, he is so irritating. It was Henry, Sophie, Ruby, Malic, Chris and me and we were waiting for the rest and playing cards as we did so. We didn't expect visitors that night, we never did and the visitors we got were a surprise that was unwelcomed.

"It's in here," Alec came in with ten burly looking men each carrying four sacks of soil with them.

"What are you doing in here, Alec?"

"That is *Sir* to you," he pulled me by the arm and practically threw me across the room, Chris caught me but fell down himself, he wasn't particularly strong, "Don't worry, I won't tell anyone about your passageway."

"How do you..."

"Do you really think I'm that naïve, Emerald 2.0?" He wasn't Alec anymore, the dashing Alec whose eyes I could swim in had vanished. He was exactly like them now. Before I had thought he was different from those heartless butchers and now that I rejected him, he's just the same; no, he isn't because it's not him. He's been replaced by one of those murderers, I can see it in his eyes, the lust for knowledge, to unravel the world's mysteries. His colour is faded and pasty, his hair is thinning to grey and it shouldn't be.

"The hole is under those two floor boards." Damn, he knew everything, he had always known everything and now we'd gone too far.

Four of the men ripped away the boards then five of them took one sack each and opened it.

"Sir, there's a child climbing up the ladder," it was Jasper.

"Just fill the hole," Alec demanded.

"He'll die," Sophie cried.

"Better than going to the experimenting labs and dying there, fill the hole."

If five sacks of dirt were to pour on him he would surely die from the impact or suffer an injury.

"Please, Alec, don't," I shouted.

"Fill it," he roared and they did. We saw the soil power down on him sack after sack, crushing a fierce blow onto Jasper, we watched his body sink into the dirt, we watched it tumble and roll to the soils command. He was flung to the bottom and mangled like a toy doll, it affected Sophie the worse and we all knew why, they had become strangely attached, but now he was gone, buried alive in a soil grave, he would forever rest underneath our feet.

"Jasper," Sophie cried.

Alec left, along with his burly men.

"Jasper, no, no, God damn it, no," Sophie clawed at the soil and began to dig as best as she could, it was useless. Sophie has never said the Lord's name in vain until now.

"Stop it, Sophie," Chris held her back, she would surely dig to the centre of the earth to find him. "He's gone."

"No," she cried, "He can't be dead, he can't, he just can't, he promised, he promised, God damn it, no."

If there is one.


"Alec, what about the others?"

"Please knock before you enter, and wait for a reply."

"What's going to happen to them, Alec, what have you done?"

"When they get caught, and they will because they have nowhere else to go, they will be taken to the experimenting labs."

"No."

"I didn't do this, Emerald 2.0, you did. If only you had quit when I said to, everything would be fine, and you'd be mine."

"I don't want to be yours."

"What if it was me or the experimenting labs, would you be mine then?"

"Bastard!"


A month has passed by, no sign of Rose, Luke or Lucy. Please let them be safe, please let them have found a safe place away from the experimenting labs, far away. Just a month and I'm already going insane, I always thought that I'd rather be in here than out there, I was wrong; I wish to God, if there is one, that I was out there. The air out there has a sweet honeysuckle taste to it, whereas the air in here is smoky and bitter.

I had had enough, I took my larger rucksack and packed essential items, a map, deodorant, clothes, a small pocket knife and other things I thought I would need.

"What are you doing?" Ruby was the first to notice, we were sleeping in the boy's room lately, the thought of having Jasper buried underneath our feet scared us, especially Sophie.

"Escaping."

"What are you talking about, Tanya, you can't escape."

"Just watch me." Ruby ran over to Chris, as if he could sort me out; he was still irritating me, just leave me alone, Chris.

"Green Eyes."

"Don't try and stop me, Chris."

"I'm not going to, I'm coming with you." Crap.

"What? You're both crazy. Sophie, Malic, Henry, get over here, now!" Ruby shouted.

Henry would not stop us; he would join, if I knew him, meaning Ruby would join too, and usually Malic.

"You can go to your death but I'm staying here," Sophie protested.

"You're more at risk here than anywhere else."

"I'm staying with Sophie."

"Malic," Henry started.

"Just leave it," Malic said, "be safe."

Alec obviously didn't know that we always had a way out, the passageway was our main way out and in but there was another way out, just out, though and once you were out the only way back in would be the passage that was now blocked. It was a slipway in the girl's toilets, another reason why we didn't use it that much, Sophie pulled up the tiles and one-by-one we went down the large metal slide into the honeysuckle world outside; how I had missed it so much. Then Sophie covered the tiles and went back to her routine. I was wrong, we had less freedom, meaning it was us that were the drones and not the people on the outside of Talent School. 1032.

What to do now? The world is an open book, I suppose; no doubt Alec will find out and send the authorities after us. Let him, he can throw anything he's got, the murderer, no, the butcher.

"So what now?" Ruby moaned.

"Now we find a place to sleep, there's an old abandoned warehouse not too far from here," the expression on her face told me she was displeased. "Come on."

We could stand staying in that warehouse for no longer than two days; it was cold and eerie, even with company. Chris would cuddle up to me and I wanted to recoil; I wish he had stayed in the school instead, in fact, I wish all of them stayed, I'm just putting them in danger.

Five days, five days is how long we've been out here and that fresh air and crisp atmosphere that was once a dream is now, slowly, turning into a nightmare. I miss the comfort of a warm bed and washing, I haven't washed in a while. The warehouse has a room with a sink so every morning and night, me and Ruby scrub ourselves down as best as we can, we're not sure about the boys, I suppose they don't mind being a little dirty. He keeps saying we'll get a cheap, low-down job that you don't need knowledge for, then we'll rent an apartment and live in it. I can hardly think it's that simple though and I don't want to live in an apartment with him, I don't want to be anywhere near him, everyday he seems to become more and more irritating, as if the debonair charm he once had has been replaced while being in the experimenting labs, replaced with just... irritatingness.

I'm wandering around the streets and it's pretty late at night, midnight to be precise, and in a way I'm relaxed. The street lights make the cold night circle in the most romantic way, if Chris was here with me now I'm sure he'd tell me that; damn, he's annoying. It's a full moon tonight and I half expect a werewolf to attack me; it's strange how people's minds can wander when they're taken away from society for just a short period of time. I'd only been in that school for two years and before that I'd been forever in this outside world, yet I and everyone else in the school seemed to think that this world was strange and that we were the normal people, we were wrong. We were the freaks, trapped in a creative cage, monkeys made to entertain, to dance, used for their advantages, slaves. If only I had noticed this sooner, I would have hidden my talents every writing essay for English that I'd get I would purposely make it terrible, there are no programs on writing creatively. Yes, there are programs on how to use correct punctuation and sentence structures and I'm guessing that's where some of my story structures came from, however the real heart of stories is the idea, the imagination, it's a talent that you're born with.

I haven't seen any sign of Luke, Lucy or Rose, my guess is they're being hunted down and I'm sure we are too. By now word will have got out and the authorities will search and if they catch us, we will go there to the experimenting labs. We often hear the sirens of police cars passing by, 'they won't find us' I whisper, but I'm sure they will soon, I'm sure they will.

The air is cold, it's strange, the air on the inside of those walls was always warm; I don't know why, it's not like the whole of Talent School had a dome over it. The moon is so full and bright, I've never seen it so full before, it seems close and I want to reach out and touch it, perhaps I could take a piece and show the others. I'm hallucinating, food isn't exactly plentiful these days, when I think of all these downsides to out here I think about going back to Talent School. 1032. Then I make myself think of Alec and I disagree straight away, I think of his hot kiss pressed against me and it feels cold, his heat no longer sways me, it sickens me.

There's someone on the bench on the path, obviously a man as seen by his slumped posture and splayed out arms; he threw his arms over the back of the bench and had his leather jacket collar turned up. Just ignore him and walk on, turning round would make it obvious, just keep walking. As I pass him I can see his head turn up but I don't look. I don't want to encourage weirdoes, just keep walking. He's following me, I'm sure he is, just keep walking. If I run, so will he, just walk in a circle back to the warehouse, one man won't be a match for all of us, just walk. His pace is quickening, I should quicken my pace too, a fast walk, just keep walking quickly, don't stop, don't look back it will encourage him, damn his walk is fast.

Sirens, sirens, I swear I hear them, and lights, blue and red lights, getting louder. I turned around and so did he, sirens were definitely in the distance. Another man arrived, two men! I'm sure we could stop two of them. He was an authority, does that mean the other man that was following me is to.

"Stop there and put your hands up!"

No, they've found me. I have to run, I must run but I can't. Why won't my legs move? *Move, come on, move.*

"Shit!" the man shouted and it wasn't a man it was a boy who had been following me. He started to run in my direction, *run, Tanya, run.* He grabbed my hand and then I was running, as if his energy had suddenly passed to me.

"Run," he shouted and then I realised who it was, that boy. *It's that boy and in the moons radiating light, his ash-mauve eyes shine brighter than the flickering street lamps and the moon itself.*

The authority pursued us and he continued to drag me by the hand, my hand, he was holding it; this strange-mysterious boy was holding my hand. Had we not been running I would have surely fainted from wonder; my heart was racing faster than my legs were moving and not because I was running away from the police, though I'm sure that had something to do with it. It was because he was holding my hand, I hope it's not sweaty; I will die if my clammy hand is moistening his.

We ran to a public toilet and the authority followed, he was five metres away. God, if there is one, where is he taking me? Why is he pulling me into a cubicle and locking the door? I want to talk to him.

"I…"

"Shh…" he held me with his arms wrapped around my hanging ones and chest, his hands resting in different places but respectively nowhere near the breasts.

I could hear the authority pound into the toilets; no doubt he would have called for backup by now.

"Come out! It's no use hiding." One-by-one he kicked in each door, one! We were on the fourth stole, two away from the side wall. The boy knocked on the wall behind us, two! He held me tighter, three!

"Hold on," he whispered, his breath still lingers in my ear.

The back wall we were resting against opened and we fell down backwards; I gasped, four!

We both slid down a metal shoot, me totally unaware of where we were going and him aware and holding onto me. I only realised my head was resting against his chest half way down the shoot and I gasped and rose my head; I swear I heard a short laugh, it calmed me. I think we were half way down, only, I couldn't see. Ouch! An impact, we had hit the bottom, luckily there was a cushion there. *Where are we?* He pulled me up and I couldn't speak, *why can I never speak?* He opened a door, how he could see in this dim light I don't know, then he hopped over a box that was in his way.

"Wait!" but he was gone, *damn it, he's gone, I don't even know his name.*

76

I was down a hill in an alleyway somewhere, it wouldn't take long to walk up and back to the warehouse, and the sirens in the distance and the lights from afar had died down. The night was silent once more and all that could be heard and felt was the warmth of his lingering voice in my ear, "hold on."

"I will, always."

I didn't tell the others what had happened.


Eight days, every day I go along the same path hoping he will be there. Sometimes I even sit on the bench and hope he'll come and ask me to move or something, anything. I want to talk to him, but what would I say, 'Hi, I'm Tanya.' What a plain name. I bet he has such an exotic name, something strange and mysterious. I've even started to write about him more, while I was in school I started a book and I knew I was writing about him since day one. I'm finishing it now, every night I write it. 'Nathan', that's a nice name. I write about this character every day; two dog tags, a leather jacket, jeans, a black top to match, impressionable facial expressions, ash-mauve eyes and jet black hair, thin, pale skin. He's my fairytale prince, he saves the day, he's a rebel and ends up almost dying but makes it through and wakes up in the new world he has helped to make, held by me, no, the girl in the book I mean, not me, Tiffany. I'm almost done, I know the ending but I haven't written it, it's almost done.


Fifteen days, I had the book secretly published by the same person that helped us last time. I didn't put my name on the cover this time, I couldn't bear to have my book taken away and replaced again. It was up in the stores in three days and apparently people liked it so no one cared about where it came from; they liked it so much that apparently there had been a break-in to a store and someone had stolen it, just one thing, my book, and nothing else. Since they sold pretty well, the person who published it got a lot of money and though we couldn't demand any back as it was illegally published, we still got £300 which would pay for clothes and food for a while, not a place to rent though and Chris still hadn't found any jobs. *Nathan where are you?* I'm so sick of Chris, he gets on my nerves constantly, I wish he'd just go away, I would dump him but he came with me and it would make things very awkward. When he cuddles up to me I want to recoil so much, so I imagine it's that mysterious boy, holding me and saving me from the authority, or was he just saving himself.

Seventeen days and I'm still taking the same route, this time Chris had decided to come with me and wasn't I just ecstatic. Couldn't he just leave me alone. "It's too dangerous to be on your own." Please. As we went past the bench, he was there, him, that boy. He looked up, meeting my gaze. Chris held me tighter. Everything was ruined, that boy knew I was marked property. As we turned the corner, I told Chris I wanted to go back. As we walked further on, I broke away from him and managed to run back to the bench, but it was too late. The boy wasn't there. I ran to the other place I imagined he might be. Bursting into the toilets I began to check the stalls, one was closed, "Looking for someone?"

It was him and my heart jumped a thousand times just to hear his voice. "Umm," I stuttered, was that all I could say, surely I had more of a vocabulary than that.

"Sit down," he ushered under the stall. I sat in the other stall on the floor and watched his hand, his beautiful hands.

"Was that your boyfriend?" Oh, great, he had already started asking that question.

"Uh, well."

"Actually I don't want to know. That way I won't have to feel guilty about the library," I heard a small thud against the stall wall and imagined him resting his head back.

"Are you hungry?"

I was starving, "Mhm."

He laughed silently. "You don't talk much, do you? Here." He passed though a cereal bar, it said 'guaranteed to keep you going for days', well, we would see.

I began to eat it in small nibbles and placed my hand on the floor closest to his stall, there he let his hand rest on mine and I tensed. His hand was on mine, I almost felt like choking on the cereal bar. If only we could touch, but this stall wall was keeping us apart. He removed his hand, I sighed but kept on eating. By the time I was finished he had disappeared from the stall, no doubt in the same way we did last time.

Twenty days, I had a lot of explaining to do when I got back the other day. I decided to take a different route this time, down the hill and around the town. The shops are full to the brim with my books, if only my name was on it. I wish it was, I wish I could change the world but what could I do now? Nothing. I would sit in a warehouse the rest of my life and marry the irritating Chris, and have irritating children called Trish and Chranya. I had written a book with a person that resembled Alec and one with a person that resembled that boy, and one with both, but never Chris. What would be the point? He would never read it and if he did, he would never realise. Then again, that boy will never read my book either, only Alec would read them and it makes me feel sick. I bet he'll know this new book is mine, he knows my work and he knows the style in which I write.

Twenty days and I'm nowhere, at first I thought I'd make something of myself. Ha, what's to make? What can I do? Nothing, that's what, absolutely nothing.

The stars are clouded tonight, as is the crescent-shaped moon that I have gotten to know so well lately; the moon was out when I saw him, when we were together.

The rain began to fall down as soon as I got to the end of the shops where the red brick wall rested with our words still on it, 'Feeding knowledge, killing cells, deadly machines of useless murderers'. Perhaps someone passes by here each day and reads those words, perhaps some local shop owner ponders it while serving the customers. Did we actually make any difference? I walked back to where the hill dipped and the road went up, water trickled down the road like a waterfall and I stopped for a while and watched it pool into the grid; it was heavy rain and the drains filled up fast. They had so much new technology and yet they hadn't solved the over-flowing drain problem. My hair and clothes were soaked, not that I cared; I had spent a little bit of my money buying myself some new items. How long would that money last us, though? A week, two? It really wasn't that much and none of us had a job. Even though I loved writing, I was not prepared to continue writing books just to get £300 or less for each one. The water trickled around my feet and ran through each slit in the ground, I felt so calm when I heard the sound of rain, real rain, not spray rain or dribbling rain, but loud, proper rain that pounded the ground and eroded every rock down to the smallest of pebbles. I could hear feet shuffling on the ground in the alleyway next to me, crashing through puddles of rain, no sirens and no lights, just the crashing of fallen water and the moving of feet. A torch shined in my eyes and I flinched and covered my face.

"Who's there?" *Don't answer, they'll take me away.*

"Over here, there's someone over here." *No there's more, run.*

"Oy!"

I ran back through the street past the shops that sold my books and back to the wall where our words lay. Why did I run this way? It was a dead end and the men surrounded me easily. I saw men in masks and black, all black, they pointed their guns towards me and held humming jelly shields up to protect themselves. From what? What would I do to them?

"Put your hands over your head and face the wall," I didn't.

"Follow the instructions," I didn't, I was too stunned with silence.

"If you don't we will be forced to shoot." Forced? Who's forcing you? Why don't you just handcuff me? *I don't have weapons or a bomb ticking in my hand, you can see that, just take me.*

"Last time, hands up," I didn't, why didn't I? *I don't want them to fire.*

"Fine, then have it your way, open fire," and they did, all the men pulled their triggers, golden bullets shot from those guns

80

towards me. The world slowed down and each bullet had a path of time behind it. The guns froze and each had a fire surrounding them; they were obviously powerful guns because they were firing so many bullets and they were loud, even in this slowed down time they were loud. Snap, back to real speed and there it was bullets piercing the rain so they could do the same to me. I was jolted to the side and pressed against the wall, only until I was in a crouched down position did I look up and see my hero's face. He knelt over me with a shield in front, similar to the ones the men were carrying except this one had no black case around it and was all a purple see-through goo that shone as the bullets reflected off it and bounced back into the men. It was stringed with blue that looked like creeping veins and made it look alive. It was attached to his wrist, unlike the men's shields, which they held. It was that boy again, he had saved me and he only took a second to glance at me, then he was focused on the men. He pulled a circular metal ball from his jacket and threw it over the shield that covered us. It beeped several times, getting faster in rhythm as it did so and flashing a small red light. It exploded and the men dispersed and ran away, if they were not already caught by it, that is. I thought they would give up after that but they came racing back towards us and the boy had already taken down his shield. He took something else from his pocket, another bomb; no, some sort of tracker and when he pressed it, a light shone from behind the men and came racing towards us, they leapt out of the way and it screeched to a halt before us. It was a rather large motorbike, a lot larger than we had nowadays. He mounted it and placed the tracker in a slot, it rumbled as he did so.

"Get on." It was either him or the men with guns, I choose him.

"Do you have helmets?" Heaven knows you would need it with this piece of junk, if there is a heaven that is.

"Ha," he laughed. I would take that as a no.

Before I knew it, we were driving straight through the men and he was swerving to dodge a flock of bullets. I held on for dear life, this thing wasn't safe, it wasn't even legal. The wind streaked through my hair and pushed at my grip, I held tight around his chest and did not dare to let go, not even for a second, or less. When we slowed down he pressed a button on his machine; now that I could properly see there were quite a few buttons. As we went down an alleyway, a large dustbin rolled out of the way and the wall parted. When we went in, it was dark at first but then a set of lights came on making the floor light up like an airport runway. He stopped and I dismounted, shaking slightly.

"Are you alright?" *No, I am not alright, I almost got killed, got on a cryptic motorbike with a complete stranger and rode it up a hill hanging on for dear life, and all of this is illegal, I'm sure.*

"Yeah, I'll be fine," *give it a few weeks.* I could speak, I actually spoke, thank God, if there is one, I spoke to him and I think I can speak again.

"You're that boy from the library and the alley, and then..."

"Yeah," thank God, if there is one, that he stopped me, I was babbling like an idiot, which is probably why he stopped me.

"I'm Jake," Jake, it was not Nathan, it wasn't at all what I expected but I liked it. It was simple, not at all like him.

"And you are?" *He wants to know my name, damn, what's my name, I know I have one it's just not there at the moment.*

"I'm... wait a minute, you kissed me." No, why did I say that?

He laughed, not a mean laugh, just a small little chuckle.

"Why? Why did you do that?"

"Spur of the moment, I suppose," Spur of the moment; did it mean nothing to him, did he not enjoy it?

"Is this what you always do, run around getting chased and going into libraries kissing random girls?"

"I don't know, do you run around sneaking into libraries writing your name on books and getting kissed by random boys?"

"Don't tease me," I demanded.

"I would never dream of it." Silence. "You know, I still don't know your name."

A door opened sideways with an exhausting puff of air, I didn't know there were doors in here, then again, I could only see black surrounding the walls.

"Oy, bro, what the hell are you doing running away from slaughters at this time of night? When mum and dad told me to look after you, they said to give you a curfew and I did. I said in by one o'clock on the dot and now it is one-o-three." Another person came in. He looked a bit like Jake but only in facial features, his hair was a dark brown and he had stubble from his chin to his neck, his eyes matched his hair and a fag hung from his mouth. He was a bit older than Jake, perhaps around Alec's age.

Jake didn't seem to be bothered by his words or the intrusion.

"Ay, who's this then? So you finally got yourself a girlfriend, ay?"

Jake laughed. "He is not my boyfriend," I stomped. I must have looked like a child to them.

"Then who are you?"

"She's a friend," Jake answered. "Now shut up will you, you'll make her nervous." It was strange but until now, I hadn't noticed the types of accents they both had; Jake's was such an amazing accent. It was obviously a pure English accent, but not the kind a rich man would acquire and yet the other man had a typical brummy accent, deepened with smoking and no doubt, alcohol.

"Well, bring 'er in then, don't leave 'er to wander."

I followed Jake and the other man down a slope and to another room where three more people sat.

"I'm Jason, by the way, Jake's older brother, but just call me Jase." Jase and Jake, not much thought had gone into separating those names.

"This is the Twiz, Techno and Pete, also known as Lauren, Taroff and um Pete."

They all seemed the same age as Jason and each one had a distinct feature about them. Taroff had a cut across his neck, blue eyes and blond hair. Lauren had the longest hair I had ever seen, it's brunette touch almost reaching to the floor, she had eyes to match and Pete had grey eyes as well as a black quiff, though he was not pale, like Jake, he was quite the opposite.

"So, you're all criminals?"

"No, we're rebels, outlaws, anything but criminals," Jason snorted. "Sure, we might occasionally steal to eat, to live, hey maybe even for a little entertainment, but basically what we're trying to do is take down the NLFS."

"The NLFS?"

"It stands for National Labs For Slaughtering," Jake said, his voice was like caramel. It rippled to and around your ears.

"Do you call them slaughterers because they take people who fail the tests after the programme and experiment on them, usually until they die?"

"Always until they die," suddenly Jason took on a serious tone which I didn't think was possible. "They don't just take people who fail the test, they take criminals too, people who go against their rules. They take people with diseases and who are near to dying, they take away disabled people as well, I knew a person who was in a wheelchair and he got taken away, then they decided to take his family away too, they take away orphans and tramps, anyone they can get their hands on. Why do you think the world doesn't have many criminals in it? Why do you think there are no people littering the streets? It's because they take them, soon enough they will go insane, they'll take everyone…"

"That's enough, Jason, she gets the point," I couldn't believe it, but he was right, the reason for all of those things, he was right; they take anyone they can get their hands on.

"So, what do each of you do?"

"Good question, good question, you see Pete here's our muscle, Techno's our nerd, I'm the weapons expert and Twiz well, Twiz is Twiz." The Twiz also know as Lauren came from behind Jason and arm locked him, something that wouldn't seem possible as he was not a weedy man.

"I'm the defence," she hissed in his ear.

"Ok, ok, Goddamn it, woman, let go!"

"And what about you?" I turned to Jake, those eyes were so mesmerising, I could stare at them all day and when I realised I was staring too much, I had to look down to the floor.

"Him?" Jason laughed, "He's the dude with the ancient teched-out motorbike and a whole lot of guts, ha."

I wanted to hear Jake's voice again, not the arrogance of Jason.

"I can see why you don't hang around with your brother that much."

"Oy, cheeky bitch," he snarled but not angrily. "Ha, ha she's a keeper this one, Jakeo."

Jake smiled, *'a keeper', what's that supposed to mean*? It occurred to me that perhaps these people, however rough or wanted they might be, might just be the answer to our problems.

"I was wondering, do you guys have any spare rooms available?"

"No need to go in any of our spare rooms, I'm sure Jakey would love for you to stay in his room," with this reply from Jason Jake slapped his hand against his own forehead.

"No, I mean, if it's alright, I was wondering whether three other people could stay here as well."

Jake looked up and suddenly all attention was on me.

"What kind of people?" Techno asked.

"Just friends."

"Same age?"

"Yes."

"We're not a babysitting club," Twiz snapped.

"Calm it, Twiz, let's hear her out, will ya?" Jason smiled, "Continue."

85

"We're situated in a warehouse at the moment and we don't really have anywhere else to go, we tried to go against the authorities before but it didn't exactly turn out so well."

"Why?" Jason puffed a ball of smoke. "What did you do?"

"They spray canned messages on walls, shop windows, spread out leaflets, that sort of thing," Jake half approved of the plan is what I got from him answering, but I don't think his brother did.

"What message?"

"Feeding knowledge, killing cells, deadly machines of useless murderers."

"No wonder it didn't work, it's too... er, poetic, people are simple-minded, should 'av just written 'knowledge machines will kill you' or somefin' like that. Like I said, people are simple-minded."

"The only one who's simple-minded is you," The Twiz laughed. I agreed, he wasn't at all like Jake, not that I could judge, I hadn't exactly known him for long.

"Baby stuff then, what went wrong?"

"They found out it was us, or rather one person did, and blocked up the passageway we used to get in and out."

"You all got out then?"

"There were ten of us."

"Oh, Goddamn sons of bitches," Jason snarled again and this time it was angry, but not because of me. "Where did you escape from again?"

I was waiting for that question and I didn't want to answer it, not many people liked Jewel-children from talent schools. They liked their music, their paintings and their books, etc, but when it came to the actual people, they didn't like them. We were the ones who got more freedom apparently. Lies, poisonous lies, we got less freedom than them and yet they still envied us, every day they wished they were one of us. I now realise that we are the birds trapped, we all are, those on the outside will never get to see the inside and vice versa for most of us.

"I'm from a talent school, Talent School. 1032."

"A creative jockey, ey? Jakester, you sure know how to pick 'em don't you? And tell me, miss Jewel-Child, what's your talent?" Jason came so close I was afraid to answer, I'm sure he could see each glisten of sweat drip from my nervous head, he crowded me so much that his smoke poured through to my lungs.

"She's a writer," Jake answered.

Jason backed away. "A writer, ey? How very interesting." I didn't understand, *why is that so interesting? Perhaps it is just the way Jason talks.*

"Well, alright, Miss Writer, we'll help you out. Guys, get in the car, Jakeo take her on the bike."

When Jason left we went to get back on the ancient bike again, I wasn't sure if I was dreading it or absolutely enthralled with it. I was also wondering how they knew where the warehouse was at all, then again, I suppose there weren't many abandoned warehouses around here.

"You still haven't told me your name."

"You know my name," I protested.

"Oh?"

"You read it off the book in the library."

"So I did." Was he not going to say it? I bet he didn't remember*, just say my name if you know it. No he doesn't know it, he's just going to wait for one of my friends to say it.*

They agreed, they actually agreed, for all they know I could be misleading them. This could be a trap to catch them, after all, they are criminals; no, they're rebels, not criminals.

I rode with Jake on the back of his motorbike. I was less scared this time, in fact, I was relaxed. I rested my head against his back and he didn't seem to mind, neither did I, I mean how else was I supposed to hold on besides wrapping my arms around him? It's not like there were handles. It was certainly a dangerous piece of equipment, which made it even more exciting. I had to keep reminding myself that I was going out with Chris or else I'd enjoy the experience too much and when you have a boyfriend, you're not supposed to enjoy wrapping your arms around another boy.

The motorbike came to a screeching halt and swerved into a parking space, we had stopped two buildings before the warehouse and I had a good idea of why. Sirens, sirens and red and blue lights, they were everywhere. They surrounded the warehouse like ants on sugar, covering the place with the same irritating stance as an insect, vile, putrid creatures. Why, why were they here? I suspected Jake would think it was a trap now and yet he said nothing. All the times I had been surrounded caught back up on me, the library, the public toilets, the town and all the time Jake had been there; two of those times he had saved me. It wasn't him they were following this time it was us, they were going to take us to the experimenting labs. I could see all of it flashing before my eyes, the showering bullets, the bodies of innocent people, Chris and his head taken from his body and Jake, Jake. Why was I so infatuated with a boy I just met? I didn't love him, I doubt I could ever love anyone, but I did like him and I liked him a lot.

Back to reality, the police, they didn't look like regular, everyday police. They were just like the men from before and there were at least twenty of them, no, thirty-five.

"How did they find us?" Jake didn't answer; after all it wasn't exactly a question he could answer.

"I can't let them be taken." By now we were crouching behind the building next to the warehouse and looking around the corner, I got up to go but Jake pulled my arm and me back.

"What are you going to do, charge in unnoticed and rescue your friends?"

"Yes." What was I saying? Of course I wasn't going to.

"Tanya, listen to me, we can't win this, we have to wait for the others." *My name, he did know it and he just said it.*

Even though I would most likely do anything for him, I didn't want to listen to reason at this moment in time and so before he could grab my arm again, I rushed into the flurry of flashing cop cars. No one saw me, they all seemed to be inside. I wasn't aware of whether Jake was following me or not. I dodged into the room and suddenly all eyes were on me, stupid move.

"Put your hands up," *not again*. I couldn't move, they had Henry, Chris and Ruby in handcuffs.

As I did not do as they commanded, one shot at me, where was my hero? Where was my knight in shining armour? Jake came in and put up his shield to deflect the bullet. Oh, that's where. He pulled out his own weapon and shot the man, a murderer and yet I did not edge away from him and I wasn't afraid, I felt safe near him.

Soon enough the men were at us with their guns shooting and bullets flurrying, Jake kept up the shield and turned to me.

"Go behind those boxes and hide," I did as I was commanded, after all, what could I possibly do? All I could do as he dodged and swerved to shoot then duck, was tremble, all I could do was gasp as one caught him by the arm and flung him around and into a wall, and all I could do was cower while he jumped, pushed off a man's head, landed on another and kicked the previous man in the back.

The doors swung open and there stood Jason with Twiz and Pete on either side of him, I suppose Techno wasn't the fighting type.

"Back up is here," Jason shouted and pulled out two of the biggest guns I had ever seen, not that I had seen many guns before. They were huge and when he fired them they shot a million bullets in less than ten seconds, I'm sure. I was surprised when he shot wildly into the men because that was where Henry, Chris and Ruby were as well and yet he didn't hit any of them. A few of the men got up and Jason laughed, still with a cigarette hanging from his mouth. He dropped the guns and pointed two fingers forward making The Twiz and Pete lunge at the men.

"Goddamn it, that's a hell of a lot of slaughters to take in three kids," he laughed.

They were all so skilled and perfect. Pete punched and threw men almost ten metres to the side. The Twiz turned and wrapped what looked like two black cylinders attached by chains around people's legs and bodies to pull them to the floor. When one came behind her she had no trouble kicking their face, even though it was clearly a lot higher than any leg should ever be able to go.

All the men started to trigger their guns simultaneously and all that could be heard was a big crunch.

"Kill them!" One roared.

"Damn it all, they have inflator guns, bastards, run!" Jason screeched and with that Jake triggered his motorbike to come crashing in.

Pete and The Twiz defended Chris and Henry from any bullets with the same shield as Jake had coming from the thing attached to his wrist, but Ruby had been dragged away by the men and no one was defending her. As I saw the bullet inject into her, I ran out from behind the boxes.

"Ruby," she began to swell and tumble, what had they done to her, what was happening? I wanted to help her but I couldn't, her veins swelled to the surface and she grew bigger. More and more men arrived. She went from fat to thin then just fat, Jake jumped and covered my eyes, I could not see but I could hear. Gurgling, bubbling sounds then an explosion, when Jake uncovered my eyes Ruby was gone and all that was left was splattered marks of blood; it had gone everywhere, on the walls, on the boxes, and even a small amount had scraped across Jake's face.

"Take them out of here," Jason yelled and they did as commanded.

"No, Ruby," Henry screamed, he struggled to get free from Pete's grip but in the end he gave in, it was either Pete or those men.

"Come on," Jake pulled me by the hand and we got on the bike again, as Chris ran by he paused.

"Tanya!"

"I'll be fine, just go with them," then Jake rode off with me holding him just as I had before. In those brief seconds, I saw the look Chris gave to Jake, it was a scolding one, already in those two seconds he had decided that he did not like the boy who had saved his girlfriend three times already.

It was so exhilarating to be on his bike; every time I rode with him my worries were forgotten. In those few minutes, I did not think of the way Chris looked at me and most especially, Jake, I didn't think about Ruby and what had happened, I didn't think about Talent School and the people we had left behind, Malic and Sophie, nor did I think of Jasper or the others who never got back in, and Alec, I definitely didn't think about Alec. The only thing that I concentrated on was the feeling I got when riding with Jake; adrenaline, flight or fight, I was flying, flying so high. As if we were riding above the clouds and through the air streaming golden stars behind us. *He looks back at me and I smile, my short hair tumbling in the open wind. No, we're not in the air anymore, we're not even driving.*

"Tanya, we're back, are you ok?" Reality, precious, hateful reality, he was a dream and it was so easy to get dragged into a dream when I was with him, never nightmares, always dreams.

"Yeah, I'm fine."

# Chapter 5

We all got our own rooms; the place was so big, it would take me ages to get used to it. Perhaps this could be my chance to actually help, to be a real rebel. But Jake, when he shot that man and when Jason shot them. All of them have killed people at some point in their life; I would never do that, I could never look into a man or woman's face and watch their eyes wobble as I pierced their head or heart with a bullet, even if it was a monster. Chris hadn't said thank you to anyone, I had said thank you and even Henry, who was traumatised by the death of Ruby, said thank you. I don't blame him for being so traumatised, no human being should ever have to see that, especially when it's your own girlfriend. For some reason, the death of Ruby wasn't worrying me so much, I was just thankful to be out of there, away from all those murderers. I'm sure it would get to me later though, but not now and as soon as Jake came in, any thoughts of Ruby that were there immediately went, until he brought it up again, that is.

"Are you ok?"

"Yeah, course," he seemed puzzled with my answer.

"Was that person one of your close friends?" *Oh,* I slumped on the bed.

"Oh, right, Ruby, she was... yeah, she was a good friend."

"Do you need anything?" Good change of subject.

"Oh, no, I'm fine, I'm just going to have a shower and sleep." The bedrooms actually had their own bathrooms and everything, how did they ever get all this?

"You'll need a towel, then," he walked out of the door. I guessed he was going to get me a towel.

He was taking a while but that might have been because I was impatient, it was a big place. I couldn't wait, I hadn't had a shower in ages; I must have looked a state. I went into the bathroom and turned on the shower. Slowly I undressed, I watched the door in the mirror as if I half expected Jake to walk in accidentally and take me in his arms. When I was fully undressed I decided it would be a good idea to lock the door, so I did. I hadn't had a shower in so long, so long for me, anyway. It was powerful and warm, the water poured down on me harder than when it had been raining and the men surrounded me, then Jake had saved me. Jake, I wish I had left the door unlocked, but I suspect even if I had, Jake wouldn't come in. Chris would though, he would gladly pounce in and join me, he made my skin crawl and the thought of him in here with me made me shiver, even under this warm water. If Chris wasn't here things would be so much easier; I think Jake realised what he was to me as soon as he called out my name, or rather what I was to him.

When I turned off the water I could hear people talking from the outside, I had no towel, so I put my trousers and jacket back on and pressed my ear against the door, my hair dripping wet against the cool steel.

"What the hell are you doing in here?"

"Getting her a towel." *Her,* I wasn't sure if I liked Jake referring to me as 'her'.

"I can do that for her," there it was again, though I really don't care when it's coming from Chris.

"Do you know where the towels are?"

It was Chris and Jake. Chris seemed angry as I had expected him to be, he was very protective of me with other men. Before, when Henry had complemented me on my new clothes, he went furious, he wasn't the same anymore. Jake seemed calm, which I had not expected.

"Just get lost," Chris was trying to be hard, as if he could ever be.

"Out of where, the room or the whole place?"

"Don't get smart with me, just don't touch my girl." His girl? I wasn't his possession.

Silence, from what I could hear Jake had just placed the towel on the bed, then he left, it didn't take long as the rooms weren't big, the bathrooms were bigger than the actual rooms to sleep in.

I went out still in what I had put on, and picked up the towel to dry my hair, my body was already half dry.

"Hey Green Eyes," he tried to place a hand on my shoulder, I shrugged it off. "What's wrong?"

"I'm tired, Chris," *in other words go away.*

"Do you want me to sleep in here tonight?" He had changed, how heartless could he be, right after Ruby had been killed and he wanted to stay in the same room as me and I knew exactly what he wanted.

"I'm tired, Chris,"

"So am I," he said, a little more venom in his voice.

"You have your own room," I didn't look at him as I spoke.

"Green Eyes."

"Just... please, Chris, I'm really tired, I want to be alone tonight." Lie, I wanted to be held, just not by him.

"Alright, just watch out Green Eyes, the people here are shifty, I don't trust them." *Who would have thought, you're an idiot Chris, an absolute idiot, the people who saved you, you don't trust, idiot.*

The next few days weren't very exciting, Henry stayed in his room and didn't eat much as expected from him, and as expected from Chris, he snooped around and tried to stir up trouble. I slept a lot, I woke the first morning to see Jake standing in the doorway, was he watching me? He said he came to tell me that if I wanted breakfast, the room with food in was down the hall and on the right from here. That was one of the main reasons I kept on sleeping, not just because I was tired, but because I secretly hoped that Jake would be there watching me again. After sleeping for most days, I also looked around but in a less snooping way than Chris; I was so glad the place was big; it meant I could hide from him. As I saw him turn around a corner I swooped into a room, there sat Jason and stood Jake. It was a rather small room with a number of screens and computers that appeared on the wall to the front of me. I practically jumped through the sliding doors that opened by the press of a button. I don't know what they'd ever do if there was a power cut, not that power cuts were very common these days.

"Right, well, I'm going to get some coffee." Jason stretched out his arms and rose off his swivelling chair, though I couldn't see it, I was certain that he winked at Jake.

I didn't speak for a while, I didn't know what to say, and then it hit me, an apology. "I'm, um... I'm..." not a very good speech, but at least it was an improvement on me not talking at all, or would it really be better if I didn't talk at all.

"I'm sorry about Chris. He's not usually a jerk, he's just very..." I should choose my words carefully, "very... protective."

"You don't need to apologise." *No, I really do.* "It's fine." His voice was so soft, so soothing, just listening to him I was already floating away. I had to snap back.

"Umm... so, what do your dog tags have written on them?"

"Nothing special," he lifted one up, "One has my name, my brother's name and my mum and dad's name, and the other has a cross on it." He came closer to show me, I should have edged away, but instead I edged closer, forward.

"So... umm... Where are your parents?"

He paused and backed away, "I suppose they're... with God."

"If there is one." *What did I just say? How insensitive, he'll hate me.*

"Excuse me?"

"I didn't mean that, I just meant because..."

"What do you mean if there is one?" He should have been angry, why was his voice so calm?

"I... I just... because they're trying to prove that there isn't one and so... so people always say 'if there is one' when someone says..." he was just staring, "I'm so sorry, I didn't mean..."

He covered my mouth. Thank God someone did, if...

"There is one." His hand floated over my mouth and down, why was he always so calm?

"How... How do you know?"

"I don't, but if we don't believe that there is one then there is no chance of there actually being one, is there." In a way, no, but in a way, yes.

Jake you're so strange, so unpredictable, I can't analyse you, unlike everyone else.

Henry came in. He seemed to like this place.

"Exploring," I laughed, maybe it was a little too soon for humour.

"There's certainly a lot to explore," maybe not.

Jason followed with a beer in hand. I thought he was going for coffee.

"And who are you again?" as polite as ever.

"Henry, do you know what kind of programme this is?" Henry said searching the screens and computers. "How much memory does its hard drive have installed and does it have optional software input programs?"

"Ah, so you're a techno freak like Taroff, ey? My guess is you'd get along like two peas in a pod," Jason laughed. "Ha, good, you can never have too many geeks." He couldn't be any more impolite if he tried.

"Jason," Jake said sternly.

"What? Nothing wrong with being a geek, they're helpful." We all stared at him in a disapproving way, "Well, I'm out then, I'll leave all you similar-aged people alone, how old are you?"

He pointed to me and then Henry.

"Seventeen."

"Seventeen."

Then he pointed to Jake who raised his eyebrow. "Ha, ha, only joking, bro, as if I could forget your birthday, I've got you a present and everything this year. God, nineteen soon, well, see you all later then."

After Jason left it wasn't long before Henry and Jake started talking and so I left the room as well,

I didn't like to get in the way of a male conversation. But before completely leaving I stopped outside of the door because of one specific thing that I heard.

"She likes you, you know?" *What did Henry just say? And why is he saying it?*

"How can you tell?"

I pressed my ear against the door, making sure not to press against the button that opened it.

"She edges closer to you like she used to do before she started going out with Chris." *Did I ever do that? I don't remember doing that.*

"And that means she likes me?" I couldn't really tell but I swear there was a twinge of hope in his voice, it strained a little, I never thought caramel could strain.

"Pretty much, does she mumble around you?"

"Mumble?" *mumble?*

"Yes, mumble, you know lots of pauses and umms, then when she talks does she go off a little and all-in-all sound a little scattered."

"Sometimes."

"Then she definitely likes you, shame she's with Chris though, the guy's just not the same anymore, ever since he got taken to the experimenting labs."

"He was taken to the experimenting labs?"

"Yep, failed a test, doesn't tell anyone much about it or what happened when he was there. I don't ask, probably just shocked about the whole experience. Tanya's probably the only one who knows anything about it, I should know, I gave her the directions to go there."

"You sent her there?" His voice sounded like it was near to raising.

"Hell, no, I just told her how to get there and said if she wanted to see Chris then go, I thought it would be the last time anyone would get to see him and I thought he'd want to see Tanya the most. Then he somehow, miraculously, got out and was sent back to us; like I said, I don't ask."

*Speak of the devil;* Chris was coming down the hall. *I suppose I should greet him, I've been avoiding him for so long he'll know something is up.*

"Hi," how very inventive.

"Hey Green Eyes."

"Want some company?" I asked.

"No," good, "I'm just going to walk around for a bit, it's so damn claustrophobic in here; underground, no windows, it's like they're bloody mole people." *Since when was Chris claustrophobic? Who cares? He's just so annoying.* He wasn't the person he used to be, Henry was right, ever since those experimenting labs he'd changed, his personality had changed. Perhaps they took something from him, a part of his brain or something. I just wanted him back to normal.

He was slightly right though, the place was a little claustrophobic. The whole place was underground with exits going up and further underground or across. The place was a cold metallic colour and had sliding doors that edged into rooms that were either darker or lighter. Every bedroom was the same, another cold and small metal room with a bathroom that was pure white and bigger than the actual bedroom. The bedroom had a cupboard activated by a palm switch and a bed that was attached to the wall.

I suppose it was claustrophobic, but I didn't care because it was a safe place.

The place that I had now named as a haven grew bigger every day, as if someone was still building it without anyone else knowing. Sometimes there would be stairs going so far down I would be too scared to go down them for fear of reaching the centre of the earth, or further. They always went down, never up, if they went up they'd be on ground level and that's what I heard Taroff say was a 'risky move'.

I hadn't seen Chris for a while and I had lost track of Jake, he seemed to be going in one of the far underground rooms a lot and I swear I saw Chris follow him once. Chris's suspicions of Jake did nothing but grow as the days got older.

After finally plucking up the courage, I decided to venture into one of the even further down rooms where I was sure Jake escaped to. I'd like to say he'd been acting funny with Chris around, but he's just the same, still calm and still perfect. As I reached the end of the stairs, I could see Jake was definitely in the room and Taroff was as well, or rather he wasn't. He was sat behind a glass screen in a room with yet another hundred computers and switches fixed to the wall, an almost invisible door leading to this room.

"Level 9, Taroff," Jake said, taking his leather jacket off and flinging it to the corner of the room, his short-sleeve shirt let his arms hangout so perfectly, they were muscled but not body-builder muscled, just perfectly muscled. I had to remind myself that Chris was still my boyfriend and that I was with him and in no way did I, or could I, ever be with this perfect muscled armed hero.

"You sure, Jake? Level 9's a bit dodgy and you know Jason doesn't like you going on the laser level that much." *The laser level? What is that?*

"It'll be fine, Jason's gone out."

"Alright then, level 9, it is."

Suddenly I realised that this was some sort of training room and I best not step in for fear of being, well, in my case, most likely killed. It didn't seem like a training area, it was just a pure white space like so many other rooms in this haven. Jake stood in the middle and the floorboards surrounding him rose to let out what looked like poorly constructed robots out of the floor, they stepped out from their elevators and the floor sank down again.

"Commencing Level 9," the voice was neither Jake's nor Taroff's but was a type of female voice that would be included in any program to make it all that softer. The robots jolted into life and then the room seemed almost fuzzy. As if it was disintegrating and being put back together again, it fizzled and bubbled into static that I couldn't see then reappeared as Jake still there, but surrounded by people with guns and Taroff and the glass screen nowhere to be seen. I watched as the men came racing at Jake and fired their guns. Now I realised why it was the laser level, all the men had lasers coming from their guns and red streaking lights fired from machines on the wall that had not been there before. Jake was so quick and so agile, he bounced off the walls as if he was made of nothing but rubber, then steel as he hit the men fiercely. I watched him almost fly, jump and quickly punch, thrust and elbow. He had no weapons but his hands and the men did have guns, and yet it was obvious that he was winning, especially when the final man fell to the ground and the last machine tumbled off the wall. The room fizzed back to its original state and now the robots were nothing but a mangled mess of parts.

"Level 9 complete," the voice sang and then the floorboards moved again and all the steel mesh and rubbish was suddenly gone.

"I've got to go, Jake, you know how to work the other easy levels if you want to try it though, right?" Jake nodded.

Taroff stepped out of the glass screen room and commenced to where I was watching in the doorway, right near the stairs.

"Alright, Tanya," he gestured as he went past and at the sound of my name, Jake turned swiftly, a quick jolt of the head as if he was surprised to see me watching.

He smiled, "Come to train?" he said stretching his arms out to indicate the entire room.

100

"I don't think I could top that performance," I laughed as he walked closer to me and I edged further into the room to lean against the wall causally.

"Can you fight?" He brought himself so that he could have almost pinned me to the wall and placed two hands on either side to lean forward and kiss me, but he didn't, in fact,he backed away, realising that he was too close. I thought about his question, *hmm... maybe those years of karate before I went to Talent School. 1032 might have paid off, I doubt it.*

"I did a little karate, about two years ago,"

"Oh?" and his body was back again, almost too close to mine, and I don't care if it is, "show me." What a seductive invitation, only it wasn't meant to be seductive and I could tell by the way he posed ready to fight.

Fighting Jake, we'd be touching, just like when he held my hand in the park when running from the authority, just like when my arms winded around him on the motor bike; I wouldn't mind touching Jake, not at all.

I laughed and went into a typical karate stance I had been taught all those years ago, I hoped I was still as flexible as I used to be. How foolish would it look if I tried to bring my leg up and it stuck half way? I tried and luckily it rose just as far as I remembered it could, I was a little hesitant at first but after realising that there was no way I could hit his head without him blocking my attacks, I became a little more aggressive. It was fun to be that carefree again, I never realised why I gave up karate. I tried the leg kick again and he grabbed my ankle and spun me around, so I tried an arm thrust, no deal, he made an X and it hit his solid arms. The fight got tenser, for me, not him and I tried to be quicker with my jabs and throws, he seemed to be enjoying my feeble attempt as a smile lit up his already shining face. I tried another jab and he spun me round again, only this time he pulled me by the waist to do so and ducked back up again.

"Spinning is cheating," I pouted and he laughed.

"Fine, then so is head kicking," my smile grew into a grin and I jumped back close to the wall to let him follow the aim for a head kick. I knew he would stop it, however I didn't know he would pull my leg, bringing me closer to him, his arm still wrapped around the top of my leg, close to my thigh. His touch that I always thought would be ice cold was warm, even through my trousers I could feel its warmth, but this was not from lust or desire, his hands were just naturally warm. He let my leg go and without thinking his arm reached out and stroked down my arms, his look was so calm and welcoming, it made me remember Alec's look of lust and compare it. This was no look of passion; in fact, it had hardly a shred of emotion surrounding it, only that cool inviting quality that swayed you. He took his arm away and walked back five metres. I knew why he had done this as Chris came in, though I suspected he would do this even if Chris had not intruded.

"Hey, Green Eyes," he smiled and came closer to wrap around me, if only it was Jake wrapped around me and not Chris's slimy fingers touching me.

His gaze immediately fixed on Jake, "What's *he* doing with you?"

"I was training," he said, as calm as always. "Did you come down to train? Do you want a particular level put on?"

Chris smiled, a sly rueful smile, then he looked at me, "What do you think, Green Eyes, should I give it a try?"

"You can if you want, but I'm going to go up now and," damn I need an excuse, "sleep for a bit," *sleep,* "I'm a bit tired." I went straight up without a glance back. *You're an idiot, Chris, and if you think you could even get past Level 2, then you're an even bigger idiot. No, you couldn't even make it past Level 1.*

It was late at night, though I don't suppose this was very late for anyone else here. Three o'clock in the morning was the time I made out on my watch when I heard a crashing sound. I followed the noise that was accompanied by swears and curses, to the room where Jake kept his bike. Chris was there, what was he doing? He stood looking at each and every control, then stroking his finger over the buttons.

"What the hell are you doing?"

"Leaving this place," he answered.

"What?"

"You heard me, I'm sick of this cage." *It isn't a cage, it's a safe haven.* "I'm riding out of here away from this cage full of... full of freaks." *Freaks?* "Freaks who train almost killing themselves in the process." I didn't understand what he was talking about at first, but I soon realised. He had obviously gone on one of the training levels and lost.

"Riding? Chris, don't tell me you're going to steal Jake's bike."

"Shut up!" he shouted. "Don't say that damn name, he's just some murderer."

*How dare he? How dare he call Jake a murderer after everything he's done, he saved us.*

"No, he's not; he's a rebel, going against the ways of this world, just like we were."

"If you love him so much then stay here with him, but I'm leaving."

What could I do? I couldn't just let him steal Jake's bike, and how did he get the key? *How the hell is he doing this, Jake wouldn't just give him the key.*

"You can't!"

"I can, are you coming with me or staying?" He mounted the bike.

"No,"

"It's obvious who you love then."

"I don't love Jake, Chris, I just... this is wrong, they helped us."

"If it wasn't for them, Ruby would still be alive. If it wasn't for you, she'd still be alive." How could he say that? I felt all the worry and guilt of Ruby's death pile onto me, just from what Chris had said, it was as if he had suddenly thrown the blame onto me, but it wasn't my fault. I had helped us; we'd all be dead right now if it wasn't for me, for them.

"Don't say that."

"Come with me, Green Eyes," *no, I can't, but Jake's bike,* "Come with me and we'll start a new life together, just the two of us," *no.*

"I love you," *but I don't love you,* "and if you really care about me, then you'll come with me." *I care about you, Chris but I can't do this.* He pressed the key into the motorbike and it grumbled as he did so, it wasn't as calming as when Jake did it.

"Get on!" and I did, he could always control me, nothing could stop that. I mounted the bike just as I usually did only there was one major difference, it wasn't Jake.

"Hold me!"

"What?"

"Hold me, just like you hold him when he's riding." What was he talking about? "Just like you hold him and rest your head on my back."

*Something's wrong with him,* I just followed his orders, though my hands were shaking as I did so. He was being so strange and now I was scared of him. He started the bike and opened the entrance, how did he even know how to ride it? Had he been spying on Jake? We went out into the night, the same bike, almost the same experience, but not the same person and because of this, it didn't feel right. This time I thought about everything; Ruby, Jasper, Alec and him, I hated it, this feeling that pulsated through my veins, it was no flight experience, it was a fight and the further we got away from the safe haven, the further we got away from Jake, I felt more anxious, more scared. My arms were wrapped around Chris but it wasn't the same, my arms felt cold and when they were wrapped around Jake they felt warm and cool at the same time; his leather jacket cooled the stretch of my arms and his waist warmed my icicle fingers, heaven, *and this right now is hell.*

He was going too fast, I could feel the wind racing around us, around me, *Chris, stop, please stop.*

"Chris, I think you should slow down," but he didn't listen, instead he revved the engine and went faster, *please slow down, Chris, please.* "Chris, please stop!"

"I can go just as fast as him." *What?* Why was he so jealous of Jake, he hadn't done anything to him. *Chris, what's wrong with you?*

We were going to crash, I could feel it, the racing pulse of a heartbeat, the crashing throb of a screeching halt, *Chris, please slow down, just stop.* The piercing of heated rubber, the sting of a sudden jolt, *Chris, stop now!* The tumbling of an already fragile body, the shattering of crisping bones, *please,* the screeching of rounding wheels, *Chris,* the battering of two bruised bodies, *stop!* And we did. We had already stopped and we had already tumbled to the ground. We were close together and unharmed, the bike was unharmed as well. Somehow it was standing up perfectly straight right next to us, rearing to go, not a scratch on it. Chris had a few cuts up the arm and I swear I could feel blood trickle off my finger as I went to touch my cheek, but on a whole, we were fine. Bruised and scraped, but fine.

The unnecessary noise had attracted some people, they were everywhere these days and now they were here. Once again, I was surrounded, we were surrounded and it was all Chris's fault, we would have been safe if we had stayed, I wanted to stay, I wish to God I had not listened to him, if there is one. *Please, God, if you are there, send me an angel, send me an angel.*

"That's one of them," one of them, what were they talking about? "Kill him."

"And the other, sir?"

"She isn't on the list but she will have seen too much after this, just kill her anyway."

*What?* What kind of logic was that? 'Just kill her anyway' and why wasn't I on the list? Surely, if Chris is on it then I am. Alec, Alec must have done this, the bastard, I hate him for this, I hate him for everything. It was obvious that we were being hunted down and either taken to the labs or, by the mass amount of pointed guns in front of us, killed. It irritated me that I wasn't on this list, this hunting list, not that I wanted to die, but in no way did I want Alec to help me live and besides, I was facing death anyway so his help was useless.

"Aim," *please, God, if there is one.*

"Open fire," *send me an angel, please.*

I closed, my eyes, and waited for the gun shot to sound; two shots sounded, though I had expected more shots like before. Then again, there were only two of us so two was all that was needed. *Bang! Bang*! Just two shots.

*Please, God, if you are there, send me an angel... send me an angel...* and he did.

Before me was an angel who had fired two shots, ten men had surrounded us and now eight did. It was an angel I'm sure, it had to be and he stood with his guns in hand with his angel wings spread out, feathered silver from the moons luminating shine.

"Don't ever steal my bike again."

Jake, it was Jake and he dodged and rolled to shoot and take them all down. They were afraid of him, they were demons and they were afraid of an angel, my angel, Jake. There was one left and we would be free, away and free and yet, when he shot him he managed to fire in our direction. Another powerful gunshot, a thousand bullets towards us, no, not towards us, towards Chris and I watched him stand up and take those thousand bullets, everywhere. His arms, his legs, his chest, he was hit everywhere and I watched his limp body drop to the ground just as the man's did. Chris, you can't die. I held him in my arms and the world began to rain again, his blood washed away with the salty water, it dribbled off my fingers and slid into the grate below me. My wounds were already closing, but Chris's were just beginning to open.

"Chris," what could I say?

"Shoot me."

"What?" What did he say?

"Shoot me, in the head, do it and then they won't use me, they won't take my brain, I can rest in peace. Shoot me!"

"No, I can't, I just, I can't." *What is he saying? I can't, I could never...*

"Respect a dying man's wish," Jake said and gave me the gun to use.

I looked at Chris, the rain dripping off his red hair, he was himself again. Sweet caring Chris again and now he would die as he always was, he was no longer different. I aimed the gun to his head; he was limp on the floor. *Chris.*

"Look after her," he said and Jake nodded.

So close to the trigger now, so close. *You are a boy, Chris.* One last lie wouldn't hurt, one last lie. *You will live a boy.* "Chris, I love you." *And you will die a boy. Bang*! And just like that the lie floated away on the smoke that had lifted from the gun. Chris lay before me dead and it had been his last wish, to die in peace. *I will never love you, Chris, I have never loved you and I never will, but I will always need you, I will always need you, Chris.*

*Dead, he is gone, dead.* Jake caught the gun as it fell from my hand, I wish he would catch me, but I'm not going to fall, just cry. Just as the rain fell to the ground so did my tears fall too. *Sirens.*

Men came racing from the streets, cars and flashing lights spread across the town, and sirens. It was always sirens that brought me back to the past, the library, being surrounded, the warehouse, Ruby. Jake was the one who snapped me back to reality, the boy whose speech made me fall into a dream snapped me back.

"Come on!" On the motorbike again and this time it was different, it was fast but it was controlled and like always, my worries melted away.

Cars persuade us, flashing their lights and blowing their sirens to get every other car out of the way, not that there were many cars at this time of night. So it was a police chase. So fast, we were

107

going so fast, but this time I did not want to stop because if we stopped and if we slowed down, we would be caught.

There was a bridge in front of us and it was mechanical to allow ships and boats under it and pass through to the docks; it was lifting up and a boat was coming in, its yellow lights scared me and its howling horn pierced my ears. Jake didn't stop, *why isn't he stopping?*

"Jake, stop!"

"We'll make it, hold on." *No, we won't*, we would fall, over the edge and fall. He wouldn't stop, in fact he went faster. The bridge split and rose to let the passing boat through, it edged further and further apart and soon enough we were going up a slope. *Just stop!* We were so close to the edge now, just a few metres away and Jake pressed one of his many buttons displayed in front of him.

"Hold on," he yelled, and I did.

The button did nothing and I was right, as we crossed the edge we fell; we were going to fall and crash into the boat, the water, everything. We were still falling and so I closed my eyes and hoped that a miracle would happen, something, anything. I heard the sound of rockets crashing on the back of the motorbike and suspected it was breaking with the speed at which we were falling, but when I opened my eyes I was wrong, we weren't falling, we were flying, actually flying. Flying away from the bridge and away from the pursuing men and cars, we were safe. They had tried to create flying cars and motorbikes, and things other than aeroplanes, and they couldn't seem to get it right. But we were actually flying, *this thing was actually flying.* I held on tighter than I had before and I think Jake noticed; I wish I could see his face right now, I wish I could see whether he was smiling or not. After everything that had just happened, I felt great. Jasper had died, Ruby had died and I had just finished off Chris, and yet I was flying, soaring through the air. I wish I could do this every day. Not only was the wind blowing through my hair, but the clouds were too. The constant rain was no match for my joy, it almost seemed to bounce off a force field that we both knew we didn't have. Up, up, further than up and beyond; I felt like I could touch the stars, I wanted to reach out to them and hold one, *though even if I can't, it doesn't matter because what I feel right now is better than any pure light from any golden star that I can take and surely I can take it because I am so high up that it must be possible. I want to ride away to the distance and off this world and it all seems possible.*

"Jake, will you take me there?"

"Take you where?" His voice was so calm, so soothing, I could fall asleep with his voice whispering in my ear. His sweet voice, just like his eyes, but then again, everything about him was sweet, a thick honeysuckle-caramel kind of sweet.

"Away from this world, to somewhere new, take me to the moon, will you take me to the moon, Jake?"

"I don't think I can take you that far," I thought he was going to laugh or even tip me off the bike for being that stupid, but no. He was serious, every ounce of his caramel voice was serious and I knew from that serious tone that if he could he would take me to the moon, he would take me anywhere. He was so unlike every other boy, so unlike Chris and so unlike Alec, he couldn't be figured out and that's what I liked. Being a writer, I tend to over analyse things and that includes people, but with Jake, I couldn't do that. I could write about his looks and his style, but not his feelings and not what I think he would say. He was too unpredictable to figure out and that meant when I was with him, my mind could rest, and my mind could never rest.

"Then how far can you take me?" I pressed my head against his jacket, his soft, cool leather jacket. "Halfway to the moon, a quarter of the way?"

"Are you drifting to sleep, Tanya?"

"Yes," *always and forever drifting asleep in your arms, to the sound of your voice I will sway, it soothes me.*

"We will be back soon. Try to stay awake or else you'll fall."

*Falling, falling, if I was falling with you it wouldn't be so bad, as long as I could hold you while we fell then it would be fine, falling. I'm not falling but if it means I get to spend just one more*

*second with you, Jake, then I will, I will fall for you, my hero, my*
*angel, my saviour, my Jake.*


When we arrived back at the haven it took me a while to gain
my balance again. It finally hit me when I got to my room,
everything that had happened flew around my mind, everything.
Ruby's death hadn't scared me, I brushed off Jasper's death as if
he was a piece of dust and Chris' death was so recent, yet, while on
the back of that bike with Jake, soaring, I had forgotten about it all
completely, *and now it was coming back.* Their deaths haunted me,
their words lingered in my memory, I saw each one die in their
own extraordinary way; Jasper by crushing, Ruby by swelling and
exploding, and Chris? Chris, in the end, he died by my hand. It was
his last wish, to die peacefully and never be used again, to rest in
peace. I sat down on the bed and rubbed my head. *Don't cry*, all
their deaths laid out in front of me like a pack of cards and I had
played them all, *don't cry.* Jake watched over me from the
doorway; though it was close to the bed he did not come any
further towards me, I cried. It was not a loud wailing cry but a soft
whimper and I am sure that if I had turned away, Jake would not
have heard it. He sat down beside me and enfolded his arms
around me. He must think I'm so strange, to be so calm with him
on the bike and now this.

What did he want? Did he want what Chris wanted every time
he did this at night, because if he did, I wouldn't give it to him.
How could he even think that I would after what had just
happened, the selfish-arrogant pig.

"What are you doing?"

"Just holding you."

"If you think I'm going to have sex with you, then forget it."

"What?"

"I mean, how could you even possibly think I would do that
after what has just happened?"

There was a long pause – a long, droning pause – where his
eyes dug deep into mine and I realised how idiotic I was.

"I don't want to sleep with you, Tanya." *I must sound and look like such a fool.*

"Call me Green Eyes."

"No." *Please.* "Chris called you Green Eyes, I am not Chris."

"I..." How could I answer to that? *He was right, he wasn't Chris, Chris was dead and right now I needed him.* I didn't love him, but I still needed him.

"I was just trying to comfort you, I would never try and use you, Tanya, never." Silence, silence and an awkward shuffle. "I should go." He got up and walked away, why had I said that? I was a damn fool.

"Wait, Jake..." Too late, he'd gone.


The next few days were silent. I told Henry everything that had happened and his reaction was not the same as it was when he had seen Ruby die; second-hand news was never the same. He stayed sombre for a few days but all in all, it didn't get to him as much as it got to me; he could socialise, he helped with odd jobs, whereas all I could do was stay in my room and wonder. I didn't go outside, that was where Chris had been, the fool. If he had stayed he would still be alive and he would most likely still be irritating me. *I wish to God, if there is one, that I had not been so stupid with Jake. Everything was fine and then I made a complete ass out of myself, he must hate me, I would hate me.* I didn't see him around the place that often but I knew he didn't go out because I would check to see if his bike was there; sometimes I didn't like to check because it felt like that night when I was with Chris and he was stealing the bike.

"You haven't been out in a while," Jason puffed a large circle of smoke into the air; *I don't think I have ever seen him without a fag in his mouth.*

"I don't really feel like going out, though if you keep smoking I might feel tempted to."

"Alright, alright, I'll put it out. God, why does everyone have a problem with me smoking around here?" He stubbed the cigarette out on the wall and dropped it. Even though I have no doubt that he always did this with his used cigarettes, I had never seen any stubs around.

"Get'n Jakester anything for his b'day?"

"I wouldn't really know what to get him, besides, I don't think he'd want a present from me."

"Ey, why?"

"He hasn't told you?"

"Told me what?"

"It doesn't matter." So he didn't tell anyone how stupid I was, not even his brother. "What are you getting him?"

"I usually get him a new gun."

"Well, I don't think I can get him something like that. I think I'll go out."

"Alright, then, and by the way, if you did something to offend Jake I don't think he'll be mad at you, he isn't the type to hold a grudge."


I ended up getting Jake a present for his birthday but I was still contemplating whether I should give it to him as I wandered the halls. I hadn't wrapped it very well, it was in a small-black box with a silver bow on the top, covered with silver tissue on the inside, but all in all, it looked pretty pathetic. I saw him in the hall as I was walking. *What do I do? Do I give it to him? No, he'll hate it; no, yes, no, damn it, just give it to him!*

"Jake," he turned around, thank God, if there is one, that he turned around.

"I…" *No I'm sure I can speak to him, I've done it before.* "I… got you a present, it's just a small thing, if you don't like it, you don't have to keep it. I mean it's just a small thing, it's not even a… I would just…" He placed his hand over my mouth and smiled. I

112

didn't realise he had gotten so close to me, I wasn't paying attention to him while I was blabbing.

"Thank you," I handed him the present. I felt like running away. If he hated it, what would he do? What if he didn't like it but didn't want to hurt my feelings? *Oh my God, if there is one, he's opening it.*

It was placed in the middle of the silver tissue paper almost shining as bright as the other tags around his neck. He pinched it with his thumb and forefinger and read it. 'My hero, my angel, save me, always.' *How stupid, how cheesy, how corny, he'll hate it.*

"Like I said, it's only a small thing and if you don't like it…"

"I love it, thank you."

Silence, his eyes still read over the text engraved on the tag, his sweet, powdered ash-mauve eyes. He took off his chain and slipped the tag onto it. He likes it, thank God, if there is one, he likes it. I know he does because if he didn't, he wouldn't wear it, he'd make up an excuse and say something like, 'oh, I misplaced it,' or 'I forgot to put it on,' but he liked it and he's wearing it.

"Jake, I… I'm sorry about the other night."

"It's alright, you were just frustrated because of Chris," he put it so bluntly, "anyone would be."

"Yeah," I was distressed but I also think I was arrogant and it wasn't completely because of what happened to Chris, not really.

"Do you want to get out of here?"

"Huh? Oh, I don't know, I haven't been out for a while."

"We could go anywhere you want."

"Don't you think you should decide? You are the birthday boy, after all." *Anywhere.*

"I don't really mind, but if you have anywhere you want to go?" *Anywhere.*

"Well there is somewhere." *Anywhere.*

"Yeah, where?" He stepped closer to me, but not too close.

"My old house, maybe to see my family, I haven't seen them in two years so I'd like to see them." 'I'd like to see them,' that's the understatement of the year. I haven't seen them in two years, Talent School. 1032 isn't very happy about visitors; in other words, when you get taken the rest of your life is gone, forgotten, ended. 'I'd like to see them', *I'd love to see them.*

"Alright, then, we'll go there."

"Are you sure? I mean, it's your birthday so we should go somewhere that will make you happy."

"Will *you* be happy if we go to your house?"

"Yeah, I would."

"Then we'll go there, because if you're happy then I'll be happy."


Up the hill and across the old road, through the dust path and into the colder sack of houses. Up the hill, through the gap and stop at the row of four houses, mine was the one on the left, one over. I still remembered, I would never forget. As I got off the bike I walked slowly towards the house, the neighbourhood was quiet and all that could be heard was Mr McRiner mowing his lawn. I remember him well, every year at Christmas time he would buy us Advent calendars, even when I got too old and my mum insisted that he didn't. The house was exactly the same as before, the archway that was rusted and broken where my sister, Isabel, cut herself, the pond that my brother, David, fell into and my bench. My glorious bench, I always used to sit on that bench and write; it would fuel my imagination and I remember once, when it was raining, I begged my mum to let me bring it into my room, she didn't let me. Yep, everything was the same, except there was one noticeable difference, a For Sale sign, no, a Sold sign.

"What?" Jake had just dismounted his bike as I said this. Why was it sold? Where were my family?

"Why is it sold?"

"Oh, the old Greyners, ey?" Mr McRiner stopped mowing his lawn and leant over the bush, "Yep, they moved not too long ago, said they needed a change."

"Where did they move to?"

"Somewhere south, didn't really ask for details. I won't be going down to visit in this day and age."

I went over to my bench; a green, small bench that was rotted and flaked from constant weathering. I sat down and sighed. They weren't supposed to leave, they were supposed to wait for me to come back. Jake joined me.

"You know, we could find them, it wouldn't be hard. We could find them and go to them."

"No, it's fine. I'll see them again, I'm sure, just not now. They were so shocked when I was taken to Talent School; mum always said I had a talent and it didn't occur to me that this talent would get me taken away."

It was autumn and the crisping leaves blew over the grass like blown dust, their orange and brown colours brushed the green and crashed into the bushes they swayed to. I don't know why this bench sparked my imagination, it just always had and now, once again, I felt invigorated.

"Do you want to go somewhere else?" Jake asked. I leant back and closed my eyes, swinging my legs forward as I did so, but as soon as I had closed my eyes, Jake pulled at my hand.

"I can't think of anywhere, just here on the bench."

"Come on, I want to show you something," Jake grabbed me by the hand and pulled me away from the bench.

What was it? I went with him on his bike and it took a while to get there. We ended up at an old building that was higher than the rest, it was abandoned and though I would usually feel wary, I went with him to the top. As we emerged from the stairs, I saw the reason why he had brought me here.

"Just in time," he said.

The sun was setting on the horizon over the other buildings and as it did so, all of the windows from each and every building caught its light. They emanated a golden beauty that could only be seen at dusk, when clouds streamed over the golden circle the windows turned to shades of pink and red, flourishing in colour at the rays touch. The gaps between buildings poured finishing lights onto streets and opening up the alleyways as yellow streams of beauty carrying the last of the sun's light to the streets. A flock of birds flapped passed the setting scene and portrayed their shadow over the sky. The light poured to everywhere at this time and made the world look golden, it made this world which was so cruel, that was so terrible, shine. Now I knew why Jake had taken me up here, everyday for a few minutes the world was good and shining from this rooftop; where all was once black and cold, it was now warm and light. Thank you, Jake, my angel.

"This is why I brought you up here. This is where my imagination sparks, when the golden light hits the shielding buildings and spreads to make the world seem good."

"It's beautiful."

"It is and yet, today, I can't seem to focus on it."

I could, it was so beautiful, so pure and when Jake went to the edge of the building, he, too, was shown in a golden light, but he always was, I swear he always was.

"Jake?"

"Yeah?" He stayed watching the sun set and I did too.

"What happened to your parents?"

Silence.

"I'm sorry, I shouldn't have…"

"They were in a car crash, the doctors saved them but they went into a coma and then, one day, when the doctors said they were getting better, they disappeared; they didn't have a funeral, their bodies were used for experiments."

"They were taken to experimenting labs?"

"Yeah, then me and Jason became orphans and they took me first. They did small tests at first, MRI scans and EEG's, but they were getting ready to do something big. I could feel it by the way they looked at me, their eyes filled with questions, as if my brain, my body, was a gold mine and they wanted every part of it."

"Jason saved me and we ran away. We found The Twiz, Techno and Pete and formed a group to fight back. We started off like you, with minor stunts and later, as we grew, we realised there were more like us, so we got in contact. Now there is a worldwide group, all just like us, communicating regularly."

I went behind him and held his hand, what could I do? I hadn't seen my parents for two years but his were gone and what was worse is that they were taken and experimented on when they could have survived; the world was turning to monsters. We stayed watching the sunset and when it went down and the last glimpse of light flashed the world from golden to black, I hugged Jake from the back and whispered in his ear.

"Happy birthday, Jake."

When we rode back I felt tired, as if watching the golden light pour over the world had strained my eyes and made them heavy. It was so soothing to rest my head against Jake's cool leather jacket. I swear I was falling asleep. Only the sudden jolt awoke me and the realisation that if I fell off it wouldn't be comfortable and I may get seriously hurt. But when we were close to the entrance, I closed my eyes. The next thing I remember I was in my room on my bed, the day's events no more than a memory that might have well been a dream because they wouldn't happen again.


He was still wearing the tag the next day, and the next day, and the next day. *Why does it make me feel so happy when I see him wear it? Why does it make me feel so happy when I see him? I've never had this feeling before, a strange sickening feeling that I don't want to go away and it comes every time I see him, every time he is there, every time he is anywhere.*

"You coming to the meeting room?" The Twiz pulled me by the arm. *Well, of course I'm coming, you're dragging me there.*

I answered but only so she'd let go and let me walk on my own.

"What's happening?"

"Taroff's got an idea."

# Chapter 6

The meeting room was a large rectangular room with a board at the end of it, opposite to where the door was. There was a large rectangular table in the middle of the room with chairs placed around it. There were various scribbles and doodles on the board and Henry and Techno were standing either side of it. I suppose Henry had sparked some sort of the idea. I sat down where there was an available seat, it wasn't near Jake but it was opposite from him and just seeing him was enough.

"The plan has eight parts to it."

"Bloody hell, eight parts, make it short and simple, why don't you. God, can I go then?"

"Jason," Jake said.

"Fine, but if I fall asleep while you're telling the amazing eight-step plan, then don't blame me."

"You're supposed to be the leader of this group," The Twiz argued.

"Doesn't that mean I don't have to listen to plans?"

"No," she fumed. "It means you have to listen to plans in detail and instruct us."

"Just listen," Techno slapped a ruler on the table. I'm guessing it was for that reason.

"Henry has come up with a plan and with my help, it may actually be able to come into reality. We have tried using the Golden Brain's memories before, true?"

A group of mumbles and "yeah, yeah," surrounded the place. What was the Golden Brain?

"Only problem is, we can't take the memories out, right? Because it would be too severe."

"Yeah, yeah, yeah."

"Well, instead of taking them, we overlap, we can create different variations of overlapping strengths and weaknesses from weak which is where constant flashbacks occur; medium, where they sometimes pop into dreams and are unaware that they mean anything, and strong where they are completely covered."

"Where are you going with this, Taroff?"

"Just listen. We have figured out that by connecting different pulse waves and overriding certain systems, it can cause a certain part of the machine to override the part that remembers, it can pinpoint the section of remembering in the brain and can therefore cover it with memories that would have been there a few years ago. That's how they did it before, they covered the memories of the people's past and how school's used to be, how history used to be, and so we change that and cover what was covered again."

"Did anyone actually get that?" Jason asked, as if he actually meant it, he was annoying but funny in an arrogant, pig-headed sort of way.

"I think everyone but you got the plan, Jason." The Twiz obviously didn't find it as funny as everyone else did.

"Listen, Twizzle, if you wanna sleep with me then just say, but don't get all high an' mighty with me."

"WHAT! Listen, you arrogant, self-centred pig of a man, do me a favour and go kill yourself or just shut up."

"But if I shut up then how would you hear my beautiful voice?"

"I swear, if you say one more word I'm going to strangle you with my bare hands."

"One more word. I look forward to that strangling, hopefully you'll pin me down as well."

The Twiz shrieked and had to be held back by Pete, if she hadn't been she probably would have pounced over the table to clog Jason.

"Leave it, Twiz," Pete said. "He's not worth it, stop winding her up, Jason."

Jason shrugged and stubbed out a cigarette butt on the table, The Twiz sat down, though she was twitching to twat him one.

"If we can go back to the plan."

"Yeah, yeah, yeah, just tell me what to do and I'll do it, Techs."

"The connection to the other rebels has been made, they all agree with the plan. Like I said, there are eight stages; 1) Distraction, 2) Gathering the Golden Brain, 3) Escape goat, 4) GB's memories, 5) Program made into memories, 6) The main program, 7) Replaced memories, and lastly, 8) Destruction. Now, we have copied part of the Golden Brain's memories before but we couldn't take him out of the home because they would suspect we were planning something, but this time we need to copy all of his memories so that we can use it to cover the whole thing."

Henry and Taroff discussed each stage with us and in that meeting, I found out what the Golden Brain was. It was a person who had memories of how it used to be, apparently he was one hundred years old this year and he contained everything we needed. I was told that it was fifty years ago when they started to change things and when they hooked up everyone to these machines, Taroff told me that it was fifty years ago when they covered peoples memories of the past and we were going to do the same and cover the memories of the machines. Of course, I wasn't alive fifty years ago so this didn't happen to me, but apparently they did it to everyone under fifty and then took the fifty year olds and over away; some went into retirement homes to keep to the allusion of safety and others were taken to the very first experimenting labs. The Golden Brain is a man who was fifty when these machines came in, therefore he remembers everything of how it used to be and how they brought in the machines. They say his wife was taken and so it affects him and he only wishes for things to be back to normal. Although the plan seems to have some gaps which I would like to argue, I can't say it's going to fail, then again I can't say it's going to work either. It is a strange plan but in a way, it makes sense. If our memories of the machines and the experimenting labs are covered with the Golden Brain's memories of old schools and teachers, among other things, then it should work. I hadn't heard about what old schools were like until today, they sounded wonderful. These people knew so much and rather than question how, I wanted to ask what else?

"But how do we get everyone on the machines, Taroff?" Jason asked. I was wondering too, but I had an idea of how.

"The big switch-on," I pitched in. "Once every two years, everyone around the world is hooked up to the machines, even people who don't go on them anymore and even the experimenters themselves. They place it on auto, it's so the machines can check the amount of programmes you've been on and if it meets with how many are already down and everything. It's basically a way to keep order and to keep an eye on people." I knew my stuff, too. My chats with Alec in my early years had taught me enough.

"Exactly," Taroff nodded, "that's when part six comes into plan."


All in all the plan was… bitty… you had to piece it together to make it truly fit and under no circumstances could these parts of the plan be switched around. The first part of the plan was the distraction; Jason and The Twiz would break into one of the main control rooms not too far from here, that way all attention would be focused on them, while Pete and Jake went to get the Golden Brain and brought him here; Jake was taking his bike and Pete would take the van. I asked to come and they agreed. Maybe I am of some use and they need me for part of the plan

"I just have a few questions about this plan." Jake and I were walking back down the hall, I was going to my room and he seemed to be following me, or at least accompanying me.

"Like?"

"Well the whole memory situation, I mean won't there be gaps?"

"Gaps?"

"Yeah, gaps, like if a person remembered getting a hair cut in Talent School."

"Then they'll remember getting a hair cut in real school," Jake stopped and smiled. "Don't worry, we're going to test it all out once we've got the Golden Brain's memories and it will work, we tested it before on a slaughter with a small ounce of the Golden Brain's memories and we covered up a memory. In that memory he got his beard shaved but when he woke up, he didn't say anything about the beard that he didn't remember having, these gaps seem to fill themselves."

"They fill themselves?"

"Yes, you see, even though the human brain is a very complicated piece of work, it also doesn't like things that aren't natural, it doesn't like 'gaps', and so any gaps that there are usually get filled."

I realised after walking that I had passed my room a while ago and was actually following him to his room; I'd never seen his room before and I wanted to see it, though I doubted it would be any different from all the other lookalike rooms in the haven.

It was the same; there was a bed, a cupboard and another door going into a bathroom, only next to his bed was filled with writing, angry letters to the slaughterers, perhaps, no, they were just... writing, stories, poems, words. I picked a piece from the wall and read it, it was good, far better than anything I'd ever written, I'm sure.

'Death from slaughters, useless ways, our deaths will be their downfall, when we die what slaughters will they butcher, no more meat to hack, then soon they will turn to each other and see meat stand before them, one by one they will kill to learn and one will be left standing, then he will turn on himself'. It was so true and things like this were all over the wall, as well as other pieces of writing; it was beautiful.

"You're a writer?"

"Sort of."

"But writers get put into Talent School." I picked another piece of paper from the wall and eyed it up and down. I had to admit I was pretty jealous, his work seemed far better than mine.

"I didn't want to be separated from my family, so I hid whatever I had and I didn't try at school." I wish I had done that, he was so much smarter than me, so much better at writing, how could I amount to someone like him? I wish I had done what he did, then maybe I would be with my family right now. Then again, if that had happened, then we would have never run away from Talent School and Henry wouldn't have left either, meaning that they would never come up with the plan and that would also mean I would never have met Jake.

"It's really good," I picked up another piece. "They're all amazing."

"They're ok, but they'll never amount to the many books you've had published."

"I doubt tha…" Wait how did he know that I'd published many books? "How do you…"

"When I saw you signing the books in the library with your name, I got Techno to check the main database and records. We typed in your name and it came up with a lot of books." A lot, now that's got to be a supreme use of a hyperbole.

One question suddenly strung across my mind, however this was a question that would just put another dot on the 'sticking my foot in my mouth' board. *Don't ask the question, I have to ask the question, I want to ask the question.* "Have you read any of my books?" *I asked the question. Damn, why did I ask the question, of course he hasn't read any of my books.*

"Just one," he's read one. He reached into the cupboard and brought out a book. "This one." It was the last one I had written, the one that was illegally published and the one that wouldn't be on the database, and yet he still knew it was mine, he still read it.

"You read…" He read the book, the book where the main character resembled him, no, it didn't resemble him it was him, but with a different name, Nathan. Nathan, Nathan, Nathan, , a name

124

that wasn't his but it was him, *in this book, this stupid, stupid book he read.* "This book?"

"How could I not?" we were sitting on the bed by now and he edged closer, funny how in my ranting I had forgotten to pay attention to movement. "I mean, it's not every day a book is written about you." He knew, Goddamn it, if there is one, he knew, how embarrassing, *he must think I'm so weird, of course I'm weird, it's like practically announcing that I like him, that I dream about him, that I'm infatuated with him, and I am.*

"It wasn't exactly you... it might have resembled you slightly..."

"Jet black hair, a leather jacket, two dog tags and sweet, powdered, ash-mauve eyes, remind you of anyone?"

What was I going to say, those features just happened to pop into my head and it wasn't really you? Of course, it was him.

"Did you like it?" *What? What kind of question was that? He must hate it; it's something a stalker would do.*

"Yes, I did," *thank God, if there is one.*

"Do I really have sweet, powdered, ash-mauve eyes?" *Yes you do, and I could melt in those eyes, I could drown in them, swim in them. They're hypnotic, looking into them makes me want to sleep and stay awake at the same time. So I can stay awake with you.*

I gulped and my eyes widened, he was staring straight at me and it was making me nervous, and at the same time, it was making me calm. His hand edged closer to mine and lightly folded over it.

"Yes," I breathed and I wish to God, if there is one, that I had not breathed it because that 'yes' was so heavy with desire, so swayed by his eyes, his touch.

"Then I have one question for you, Tanya." *Yes, anything, any question, anything.* "Are we going to change the world?"

*I hope so, I really do.* "Yes."

He smiled, what did I expect to come after that smile? I remembered every smile Chris had ever given me and it had always wanted something and I had always given it. What did he want? Did he want anything, a hug, a kiss, anything? *I swear, I would give it to him.*

"The plan starts tomorrow, are you nervous?"

"A little."

"Then you should sleep."

"Where?" *What a stupid question, why did I ask that? Did I secretly want to sleep here, with him?*

"Where?" he repeated, as confused as me. "Anywhere," he smiled.

"Where do you think I should sleep?" *Another stupid question, another ridiculously stupid, idiotic question.*

"Here." *What? Here, did he say here? He did, he wants me to sleep here, in his room, with him and I want to as well.*

"Here?"

"Do you want to?"

*More than anything in the world.* "Yes, do you want me to sleep here?" *Please say yes.*

"Yes," no hesitation, no pause.

*So what now? What do we do?* At first, we sat there, our answers still ringing in each other's ears. Then, he brought his hand to my face and stroked away the misplaced hair, his hand rested on my cheek and I closed my eyes and relaxed. I lay down on the bed and he followed my actions, he enfolded me in his arms and stroked me from the neck downwards while keeping one arm firmly wrapped around me, as if he never wanted to lose me, and I never wanted to lose him, never, *my angel.* I fell asleep to his gentle stroking.

We just slept.

Jake and I were to go in and speak to the Golden Brain. Jake assured me he would come with us because he wanted things back to the way they used to be. The care home was small and had very few people in it. Jake told me that one of the reasons he would never be taken is because of his age, a man of one hundred doesn't have a brain that can be used to advantage, or any other body parts for that matter. At least, to the slaughterer's knowledge; to us it was extremely useful.

"Hi, I'm here to visit my grandfather, Patrick Merdaisy." Even Jake's lies sounded sweet, it didn't seem right lying to a nurse though. The front desk was modern and to the nurses taste. However the living room was full of old pictures and portraits, nothing that could hint back to how things were, only sweet little reminders of what will never be again.

"He's just through here, to the left."

"Thank you."

Patrick Merdaisy was, in short, old. He had a beer gut from nights at the local pub after work and a receding hairline just from age. I was surprised it wasn't all gone and yet, small, thinning lines of it still sat on his black head. He had bags under his eyes that looked like they had in them the very stories of time; liver spots surrounded his face and bare knuckles. Long hairs grew from his drooping ears and growing nose, and his teeth were stringed with beef from last week's meal and stained with antique yellow. He looked worn and tired and if he closed his eyes for more than a few minutes, he would surely keep them closed.

"Hi Pat, it's me, Jake."

"Jacob," Jake winced, he obviously didn't like being called that, after all, it wasn't his real name.

"Yeah, we need your help."

"Who?" His voice sounded like it hooted every word loudly, as if he needed to shout so that the sound would reach his ears.

"Me and Jason,"

"Jacob and Jacky need my help."

No, but it would do.

"Yes, we need your memories again, remember your memories of how the old days were?"

"Yeah I remember, you got the thingy-ma-jig. Can't take memories if you ain't got the thingy-ma-jig."

"Won't it hurt him?" I asked, "Taking away his memories, I mean?"

"What? Speak up, I can't hear you..."

"No, it doesn't really take them away, it just sort of replicates them."

"So, where's the thingy-ma-jig Jacob, do ya have it?"

"No, we need to copy all the memories this time, Pat; we need you to come with us. If we can get all your memories it can help to change things back to normal."

"Normal, ey?" He considered. "Well, alright then, where's my walking stick?"

I handed him the walking stick that leant against the wall and he started to shuffle, at this rate we would be at the van in a year.

"You know what to do, right?"

"Yeah." I had to distract the nurse while Jake got him outside and there Pete would be waiting in the van, Jake and I would catch up on the bike later.

"Excuse me," I went to the side of the desk so that her attention was focused away from the door. "I was wondering if you could locate someone for me, only, I thought they were in this care home."

"Alright and who is this person?"

"My grandmother, Bertricks Agnes Penelope Tawnsworth."

"Alright then," I couldn't have thought of a more fake name. "I'll just look on the computer to see what home she's in, has she been recently submitted?"

I saw Pat shuffle along with the help of Jake, the poor man was in his dressing gown and slippers.

"Yes, just last Thursday."

"Hmmm, there doesn't seem to be a Bertricks anywhere."

"Are you sure? She was just put in, I'm sure she was."

"Well, nothing's coming up," the door closed and Pat got in the van.

"Oh, well, I'll just have to ask somewhere else. Must go now, thank you very much, bye."

It wasn't long before the police were following us, after figuring out that we had stolen Patrick Merdaisy. The van was easy to follow, the day was light as ever and the van was pitch black with tinted windows. Our job was to follow it and make sure they didn't get caught and if they did, then we had to stop them. Jake was well equipped for the job but I had nothing, my weapon was Jake. We followed the van to the alleyway and dodged in front of the police car to give them some time to get away; we could only flash by for a second and then we had to turn around and keep on following behind the police car. I hoped we had given them enough time. We did, the van turned into the scrap yard. Scrap yards hadn't changed much; the machines had gotten bigger, meaning it only took one large metal square on a line to crush a car instantly. The van swerved and hit a machine then dodged the hammer of a crushing square; it started again and stopped as a police car came in front of it, as the police car edged further forward, the van edged backwards. Jake screeched to a halt and we watched as the van went slowly under the hammer and was crushed, the sounds of grinding and crunching spilled out over the scrap yard and now the man named as Patrick Merdaisy was pronounced dead, as well as the person who had taken him. It had all gone according to plan, as the van went down the alley we screeched in front of the police car, making them stop for a few seconds, in these few seconds the ground opened up to let the original van in and another van, controlled by Taroff and Henry that was already placed in the alley, drive on. They were placed on

129

the roof of a building and controlled the car by a wireless connection, all technical stuff that no one wanted to ask about. They led it into the scrap yard and missed the hammer the first time to make it realistic, we followed to make sure the plan succeeded. Then they moved the car back so it looked like it was backing away, to get crushed so that Patrick Merdaisy could be pronounced dead, meaning the big programme where everyone was hooked up to the machines would still go on and they wouldn't suspect anything. Two bodies were placed in the controlled van, one in the driver's seat and one in the back; two slaughters that had previously been killed, that way if they looked through any bits left of the car, which didn't seem possible, they would find bones, flesh and blood and leave it, after all, it could hardly be used now and they wouldn't bother identifying it if they saw the blood and... well, guts. While this was going on, Jason and The Twiz tried to break into one of the main control rooms to reduce the number of police that we would get; they were supposed to fail and get away and due to the success of the plan, I guessed they did. The first three parts of the plan went off without a hitch, now we just had to finish the other five parts. I didn't want to hope this time, though this time was bigger. All those times I had rebelled had been small but this was something else, it might actually work, this time the world could be changed. The world could be back to when knowledge was not fed, when people who couldn't write and sing were with others, when schools were not separated, when we had time to choose what we wanted to be and when people were not murdered for experiments. This world could change, it did have possibilities, the world would change, I knew it this time, this had to be it. Things had to change.

We all thought the plan would go off without any hitches or hiccups. It was almost perfect; every step had been plotted carefully. Jason and The Twiz were only supposed to go so far and under no circumstances were they to go anywhere near the main room, but the Twiz had gone too far.

"Damn it!" We were in the meeting room and all in all, we were trying to avoid the rage of Jason. He threw chairs all over the place, picking two up at a time and throwing them over the table.

"God fuck and shit it all, damn it!" He threw another one, then another.

"Jason, calm down," he wouldn't listen to Jake and continued to throw chairs. How could you not listen to that perfect voice?

"No, I will not calm down," another one was thrown across the room. "She was supposed to stay away from the main room, not walk right into the bloody thing. What the hell was she thinking, why the hell did she do that?" Another chair crashed against the wall behind us.

"And it's all because…"

"Jason, did she tell you to divert the mission?"

"…And it's all because…"

"Jason, did she tell you to divert the mission?"

"Of this stupid, fucking plan!" He threw his last chair over to the board and it fell down.

"Jason! Did she tell you to divert the mission?"

"NO!" he roared. "For God's sake, NO!" His tone hushed to a whisper. "She told us to continue with the plan. I'm going out!"

"Jason," Jake grabbed his arm, if anyone could get through to him, it would be Jake.

"Jake, just let me cool down, just leave me," so he did. Jason stormed out the door, his stomping footsteps echoing through the metal halls.

"Why would it matter if she had told him to divert the plan?" I asked, probably not the best time to ask but I had stuck my foot in my mouth so many times that I didn't think it mattered anymore.

"Because," Taroff started, "if she had told us to divert then we would have to, because it would be her dying wish. But since her dying wish is to continue, then we will." A dying wish, these people were far from criminals, they lived on respect.

So the plan would go ahead as scheduled, there were a few more parts to it now and with the days ageing, I grew tenser. I was

131

scared, with each growing day I felt more inclined to be with Jake, but I didn't dare for fear of me leaping into his arms and him not catching me. I didn't sleep in his room the next night, or the next, but I wanted to. Tomorrow we were going to replicate the Golden Brain's memories. Taroff told me that it would be more efficient to actually take them instead of replicating them, but we all knew that was wrong. I was so nervous and I didn't know why. If things went wrong, what would happen?

# Chapter 7

Patrick Merdaisy had been placed in the biggest room that was in the haven, which was basically the same size as any other room considering every room was completely the same. I don't know why I went to see Patrick Merdaisy, there was something about him that appealed to me. Perhaps it was his grumpy, then happy, then grumpy again, personality. Maybe it was the fact that there was so much history in his eyes and in every inch of him that I almost felt like taking a chisel and seeing if fossils rested among his bones. I wanted to learn things, about the past, his past, the one he remembered. I wanted to know what he remembered exactly, and I wanted to know what kind of golden light of the past was going to flow over us if the plan went without another hitch.

He sat slumped in an armchair; my guess is, it had been brought here exactly for him. It was a small, green and brown chequered chair, dusty and withered with age, like him. The room was still the opposite of the corridor walls colour, they were a dim grey here but light poured from the shimmering white of the halls, meaning he had no trouble reading his newspaper without the light on. I wondered for a minute why he seemed so healthy at this age, he could still read, still walk, not very well, but he could still walk. He could talk, I wasn't very good on age and when you started deteriorating, but I was sure people of one hundred didn't usually look as well as him. Yet, when I looked at him again, he did seem aged; his eyes quivered as they read even the title of the newspaper. His nose and ears were so large that I swear they took up the majority of his face, like a dying bull, his nostrils flared. His thin strands of thinning hair seemed more fragile than silver, as if touching them would cause one to fall and then another, a domino effect. His deep eyes wrinkled into bags underneath, and swallowed into small pupils in the depths of his irises. He did not look away from his newspaper as he spoke.

"Are you going to come in, or just stand there gawping?"

133

"Umm…" That had caught me off guard, people had been so nice and polite here. Even Jason with his now overflowing mood swings and the recently deceased 'The Twiz' had been polite in their own personal way. Well, sometimes.

"You're going to choose gawping, then."

"I… sorry," I advanced into the room, hoping he wouldn't send me out for not knocking or asking to come in, but he did nothing but look up. His stare was both sad and fixing; he could be an ancient animal still hunting for its prey to keep him alive.

"Well, are you here for a particular reason or do you just want to stand there?"

"No I…" I quickly moved to sit on the bed across from him, his gaze stayed fixed and small. "I was just wondering. What was it like?"

"What was it like?" He sounded as if he had never heard this question before, but I was sure that Jake or Jason or someone would have asked him, wouldn't they? No, they wouldn't have, they wouldn't have wanted to remind him of what was and what could never come about again. But things were different now, he knew they'd be different, he had been told the plan, things *were* going to change.

"What do you mean?"

"I mean, when you were younger, fifty years ago, before the machines?"

My question stayed, remaining still and unanswered, he laughed. "What was it like?" He snorted again. "Compared to today, it was gold." *I knew it.*

"We didn't think much of it at the time, until it was gone, of course. What was it like?" He considered again. "Well, what do you mean, what part?"

"All of it," I breathed, thinking of the possibilities of the past, the forgotten past.

"Well, hmm, people had a choice, in a way. School was different, we went through the motions of lessons, learning with our brains and not from machines. We had fun, to say the least. In class with friends, I'm not sure it's that much different, but, of course, there were definitely no senseless murders, there was war but there was also peace and now looking back on it, I can see all the things that were so different.

"I remember skipping pebbles across the green-streamed pool with my friends fishing on the side, our carefree days of youth were not clouded by decision, we had all the time in the world to decide our futures, no computer programme lingered over us to tell us what we must and must not do. I remember coming to my options and then having no pressure to decide what I wanted quickly, I had time to wait, there was no rush. I remember finally choosing what I wanted to be, it wasn't something fancy, I wanted to build, small things, houses, this and that. Structures amazed me, even small ones and I wanted to be a part of that. It felt so good to choose, to do something I loved and to be able to go back if I got bored. Then things changed, I had had such an amazing life. I had a wife, three kids, but it all changed, some were taken when those machines were finally put in place, some were killed on the spot. History is not remembered because they erased it from memory, me and my wife were placed in a residential home, at fifty. Fifty! My children's memories were erased, I never saw them again; maybe they're alive today, maybe they're somewhere around. But I doubt it, though their memories were erased they should have remembered me, everything else, but no, so they must have been taken." His eyes didn't well up as I expected them to, they just stayed thoughtful, "My wife was soon taken as well. I remember such an amazing life and then a war, though it may not be seen as that, it was. People were afraid, they ran when rumour got out that memories were being erased. They had taken a small group to test first and news had slipped to the media quickly. The world turned to a war, one big war, where people fought over machines and bodies, people would be taken in their sleep and everything was turned upside down, the world became a bloody fire of anguish. Soon, it settled down and everyone had been turned to mindlessness or taken. The lucky ones, me being one of them, were placed in residential homes and left to forget, as if we could forget. I'm the last, the last in that home anyway, not that I know about any other residential home. I was left there for fifty years, to

135

rot, never allowed out, just left to rot and forget. I could never forget, never, till the day I die."


Patrick's story had both scared me and made me hope for the plan's success even more, the plan made me more nervous than I should have been. I wanted that golden world Patrick had talked about. The world I was in seemed even more monstrous now.

I shouldn't have but slowly and hesitantly, I walked to Jake's room, *I hope he's there*. He was, at first I stayed at the door watching him without being noticed, but then he took his shirt off and in fear of being like a stalker again, I made an entrance.

He turned his head to my intrusion. "Are you ok?" He was so caring.

"Yes, I'm just a little nervous about tomorrow." His body was perfect, it wasn't overly muscled or rippled like that of a weightlifters body, but it was more streamlined, like a swimmer's. He had muscles, but they weren't bulging; like a swimmer, he was straight and firm. I almost considered reaching out and touching his steel-tight chest, however the word 'stalker' hummed through my mind again.

"Do you want to sleep here tonight or…" he twiddled his shirt in his hands; his leather jacket was spread out on the bed. I had been waiting for that question for a while now and I knew what I was going to say, the same thing I had said before.

"Do you want me to sleep here?" He smiled.

"Yes." I was blushing, my rosy cheeks were so visible that I had to look down and only looked up when he came over to me, and held me. My head rested on the crook of his neck and he rested his chin on my head. His body was warm as it pressed lightly against mine and my hand reached up, my angel, my hero. We stayed there for a while, just holding each other, everything was always just with him and yet, I didn't mind because it was just fine, just perfect and just enough. When we both lay down on the bed I almost instantly fell asleep, I must have been tired, after all my nights weren't very comfortable without Jake by my side. I wonder how long it took Jake to fall asleep, all I had to do was look into those eyes, those sweet, powdered, ash-mauve eyes, or have him hold me and gently I'd be rocked to sleep. I remember how I would sleep next to Chris, those nights were so restless and uncomfortable. I was always so hot but did not dare to take off the cover for fear of one of the other boys in the room seeing me bare-chested, or bare anything. Talent School wasn't very private. Here it was though, never once has anyone but Chris walked in on me, it's so peaceful here that I swear I could spend an eternity in the haven with Jake, as long as Jake was here. I would always be able to spend an eternity anywhere with him.

When I woke up the next morning Jake was still asleep, his arms gently twisted round me. I rested my hand on his cheek and smiled, it turns out he wasn't sleeping.

"Morning," he didn't open his eyes but let my knuckles graze his face lightly.

"Morning." I curled up closer to him and rested my head against his bare chest. *I don't want this morning to end, I want to be with you forever, Jake.*

He kept his eyes closed but kissed me on the head and raised his arm angled on my back to stroke my head. I had never had someone so gentle with me before, never.


The Golden Brain's memories were to be replicated and stored; to do this, he had to be hooked up to one of the knowledge machines. Taroff had programmed two machines to work this way, almost in reverse. It turns out that they had seven of these machines all in one room. This room was their main source of data and information. It consisted of the knowledge machine in the middle with seven leading out attachments, a rather large computer on the left side of the wall as you entered and a number of smaller computers and screens on the right, many showing the rest of the haven, in other words showing images from security cameras. The room seemed darker from the rest, where all other rooms seemed to have a bright metallic glow coming from white lights, this room seemed to be dimmer. It had a few bars of orange light hanging from the ceiling and all in all, it was very dim. The room made me feel uneasy, as if I was back in Talent School about to be hooked up to the machines again. Patrick Merdaisy was brought in and sat down, he didn't seem at all worried, then again, this was not an interrogation.

"Now, since it isn't like an EEG this time, Pat, we have to give you a neck scar, is that alright?" Taroff spoke slowly and loudly.

"I'm deaf, not bloody foreign, you idiot." Ha, that made me laugh. "Just get it on me, come on, hurry now, I don't have all year, for all I know, I don't have all day."

"Right," Taroff laughed and brought over the neck brace that was attached to the machine. I could feel it's cold touch resting against my neck and for a second, I thought Taroff was bringing it to me and I flinched and stepped back, knocking into Jake, he steadied me.

Pete gave Patrick the scar, the equipment for it was something that looked rather like a large drill and sounded like one to.

"This will hurt a bit," Pete started the drill. It brought me back to when I first had the scar placed in, I was so young, we all were and it hurt so much.

"At this day and age, my skin can't feel a thing, just do it, I want a long nap after this." I looked away as they drilled a hole in his neck, it went deep to the spine and somehow it didn't kill him, it never killed anyone. He didn't flinch or wince, but I did and Jake crooked his arm around me as I turned away and he looked straight at it.

"Done." Pete brought away the drill, it was dripping red. "We should clean this up before placing the brace on him."

"Oh, just do it, will you?" Patrick was certainly an impatient old man.

"Alright," Taroff hooked him to the machine via the neck brace and went to press keys, the thing he did best.

"Wait." Was Patrick having second thoughts? "It's more efficient if you take my memories, not just replicate them, right?"

"Yeah, but if we do that then you won't remember anything and at this age, you'll probably die." Taroff did not look away from the screen as he said this, he was sure that he was just going to replicate the memories, not take them.

"Do that then."

"What?"

"I said, do that."

"But you might die," I protested.

"I'm sure I will, but how long do I have left to live anyway? I had a good fifty years and then the rest were poisoned, if doing this can change things, then do it, by God, just do it!"

"Pat, are you sure?" Taroff looked up and into those ancient eyes.

"Yes, now hurry up. Like I said, I want a nice, long nap after this." He would surely get one.

As the machine was powered up, he jolted and his eyes glazed over. The computer wasn't like those of modern day, it looked old, as if someone had thrown a bunch of old car parts and artefacts together. Nowadays, everything was touch-screen, however, this computer had a keyboard and not a touch screen. Patrick's mouth opened wide and the loading bar on the screen began to fill up. Just a few more seconds. I held Patrick's wrist to feel his pulse, it was slowing, almost there, if he died we could do nothing, the pulse was so quiet, nearly done, it stopped, *done.* The bar was full and Patrick was dead; I had never held a dead man's wrist before, it wasn't scary but almost calming. The last breath of his life was whisked away, but now those withered and tired eyes could finally rest and I could feel him resting, he was at peace.

"He's dead."

"He's with God now," Jake said. *Don't think it, don't think it, if there is one.* Old habits die hard, I suppose.

Step four was complete.

"Now, me and Henry will make the memories into a programme that will cross wire the brain's memory section, causing anyone to take the programme to forget about the machines and remember the past Pat lived in. Then we will override the mainframe system, hopefully without being noticed, and cover the memory programme with our programme, then, when everyone goes on, it's done."

"Good." It was Jake who answered; even though he was younger, the others seemed to respect him. His brother, Jason, had been going out a lot lately, he had quit smoking, too, and drinking, at least one good thing has come of this so far. But I didn't think his quit habits would stay quit for long.


Each step of the plan was falling into place, one by one. Every night I got a little more nervous and a little more excited. To think this dream might actually happen, the dream that's been on the tip of everyone's mind could come true, and I would be a part of it, I would be a part of creating this dream and making it into reality.

Henry and Taroff were working on the programme and it was going to take a few days. They had a deadline, next week, that's when the real programme is uploaded ready for the switch-on.

As I grew more nervous each day, I constantly slept in Jake's room, we just slept, we always just slept. It was strange; I had never stayed in a boy's bed before and just slept. With Chris, it had always been more than sleeping, much more. Even when I didn't want to and he did, Chris and I had never just slept. Jake was so different, whereas Chris and I would go to separate sides of the bed after doing what was not sleeping, Jake and I didn't. We stayed close together all through the night as if he was afraid to let me go, and I didn't want him to let me go. With Chris, I would sometimes stay awake at night due to the heat and discomfort but with Jake, I could almost instantly fall asleep in his arms. The sensation I got when he held me was neither hot nor cold and yet, at the same time, it was both. We hadn't kissed since that night in the library and I wanted to kiss him, I really did. I wish to God, if there is one, that I could feel his electric lips pressed against mine, *I really do.*

"So, how will it work in the end?" Though I had got the basics of the plan, I was still unsure of some of the minute details. With all the questions I had been asking, Jake must have thought I was dumb, then again, it's not possible to be dumb these days what with all the knowledge that's been fed to us.

"What do you mean?"

"Well, destroying the machines?"

He didn't take long to answer, "The programme will not only replace their memories, but will tap into a part of the brain that controls sleep and make them, well, sleep for ten hours. That ten hours will then give us enough time to destroy the machines."

"Just us?" How stupid, of course it wouldn't be just us.

"Rebels, for every 100 machines in the world there are ten rebels, like us. In other words, enough to take down the machines afterwards. They've all been contacted, they all agree with the plan."

"So some will remember?"

"Yes, the ones destroying the machine, in other words, us."

"What about books?" Of course, sometimes I just asked questions to hear his voice.

"Books?"

"Yeah, they're still around but not all are in schools, like revision guides and text books for English, science, etc. And some books for entertainment, like the ones I wrote; they don't have author's names on them. Was it always like that? Won't is seem strange?"

"I already said the gaps just seem to fill themselves. It's all been tested before. We know what we're doing, it will be fine, just trust me." With that lasting statement running through my head, he came closer and held me tight.

"Ok." *How could I not trust you, you're amazing, Jake, amazing. Jake, my hero.*

Though usually when Jake held me I wouldn't think and my mind became a blank slate, tonight it was different. In a few days, the big programme would happen, but that wasn't what was on my mind. What was on my mind was Jake, I had slept in his room for a number of times now, just slept, and I had only kissed him once, in the library, and yet, I was hoping for more. Not more kisses and not more than sleeping, but more. He had never said, 'I love you', and out of all the things his caramel voice could ripple, that was the one thing I wanted to hear the most. Chris used to say it, Alec said it and yet, when they said it, I would always wince because I could never say back to them, that I loved them truthfully, because I didn't, and yet, with Jake, I yearn to hear those words, even if I'm still afraid to utter them myself.

"Jake?"

"Yes?" His breath tickled my hair and blew down to meet my neck.

"Do you love me?" What a hard hitting question, what boy would ever answer that?

"Yes." 'Yes' he said yes, and quickly as well. I should be jumping for joy and yet, I can't, not until he says those words, those three little words.

"Then why have you never said it?"

He pulled away but kept his arms gently above the crooks of my elbows. "You've never said it to me."

So, what were we doing then, waiting until the other said it, because I would surely not do it first, it had never been me first. I'm not even sure if I do love you, Jake, I don't think I can love. I like you, a lot, but love is a whole different subject. We were each playing a game, a game that neither of us would win and neither would lose.

"Yeah." Yeah, that was the best answer I could come up with?

First his eyes flinched away for a second and I thought it was because of my stale answer, but it wasn't. I saw something in his eyes that made me think, he was restraining himself, but why? Was he afraid of hurting me? Maybe it was because of Chris's death.

142

He crooked up my chin and smiled, his smile was so sweet, maybe even as sweet as his lips or his eyes, his sweet, powdered, ash-mauve eyes. "I'm just waiting for the right time, the perfect moment."

That sounded good, the perfect moment. It made me think of how Chris would just blurt out the words without even thinking about the semantics behind it. I hadn't even stopped thinking before I realised that he had brought his lips down to mine and was kissing me, and I was kissing back. Just like in the library, it was just me and him, except this time, it was better; there was no awkward squatting from kneeling down and no balancing. It was just me and him, his arm stroked against my back, while his other angled my head and I let it. Though, at first, his kiss shocked me and I backed to the wall and placed my hand against it, I soon relaxed and wrapped both of my hands around his neck. Electric, just like before, his cool lips softened mine, his lips were so cold but his beating breath was so warm, from the outside it sent buzzes of waves throughout me while his trailing breath warmed my insides, making them melt to his hot-cold kiss. Was this his way of apologising for not saying, 'I love you'? No, if it was, it would be fierce, like Chris's kiss, but this wasn't fierce, it was gentle, soft and calming, like him. I swear sparks flew from that kiss, that second magical kiss that I was given, electric. My lips stayed parted and my eyes stayed closed as he backed away and looked at me, he stroked my cheek and though my eyes were closed, I knew he'd be smiling.

He was. "I should go and check on how Henry and Taroff are doing."

"Ok," my voice echoed electric sparks.

"Do you want to come?"

"I think I'll go for a little walk outside before sleeping, if it's not raining."

"Do you want me to come?"

"I'll be fine on my own. I know you have some things to do before you can go to sleep so I won't get in your way. I won't be long." I copied his actions and placed my hand on his cheek, he closed his eyes as if my touch was something magical, a sin of desire. Then it was there again, his breathtaking kiss pushed against me, my lips smothering his. My lips were hot, his were cold, his insides were warm, mine were cold, electric. This time it didn't last as long, as I had expected, it was a goodbye kiss, for now, anyway.

He went to check on Taroff and Henry, Henry had really become a part of the team lately, he practically loved this place.

The air outside was bitter and I suspected it would be warmer if I wasn't wearing just a plain, white tank top, a grey, denim skirt, boots and a necklace that wouldn't keep me warm even if I had a thousand of them wrapped around my body. I had just stepped outside one of the stair entrances, the one with the brick code from the outside that I had memorised from day to day of being in the haven. It was a cloudy night, where the dark blue sky would be turned grey and murky. The kind of weather where owls hooted over the night sky and bats flew to their caves, an eerie kind of weather. A light flashed and covered my whole body in a florescent yellow, it was from a car light that was placed at the end of the alleyway. I could see figures standing before it but due to the blinding light, they were little but black shadows. I couldn't go back through the brick door entrance or any of the other entrances in the alleyway. All in all, there were four and if I went in, they would know about the haven, meaning everything would be found out, figured out, ruined.

Who was it? All I could hear was muffled whispering while I tried to plan my escape route. There was none, a blocked-off alley, the only way to escape was to run around the side of the car and go round to the underground grate entrance. I tried it and managed to duck and dodge past the car, there was only one car and it wasn't long before that one was following me, along with the shadows that had blocked the cars lights. I ran.

*Running, running, I'm running and if I stop, I'll be caught. but by who, who is chasing me?* I dodged down an alleyway, it wasn't the right one, the one with any other entrances, but at least the car couldn't get down it. *Run, just run, Tanya, run, don't look back, just run. A dead end, no!* A dead end and now I would be dead; if it was the experimenting labs they'd slaughter me here and now or take me away and pull my spine from my body, pluck my brain from my head and I'd die. *I don't want to die, not now, not here and not in this way. Jake where are you? You're always here when I'm in trouble, you're always here, my angel, my hero, my saviour, Jake, where are you?* The car's beam focused on me once again and the shadows from before emerged. At first, I thought they weren't human, aliens from another world come to probe and experiment on me, just like the slaughterers. I was wrong, it wasn't aliens, it wasn't experimenters, it was Alec, Alec and his burly crew, the same crew that had filled the hole. I should have noticed from their massive, shadowed appearance that it was them. Alec looked different, his eyes that were always so blue had shrunk in size and were swollen around the lids, they looked red raw, from crying, no, from scratching. His face was so pale and his hair seemed thinner and I swear I could see streaks of grey, though from the angle of the light it might not have been like that. He knew exactly who I was at first glance and I knew who he was as well. Me, perkier than ever and him drained of his energy. My guess is they hounded him for letting students escape, but what was he doing out on the streets?

"Finally," he gasped, and it seemed like such a long gasp as if I was the thing he had been waiting for forever and now he finally had me.

"Grab her and put her in the car, let's go!"

When they came towards me I struggled to get free from their burly grip but I couldn't, they weren't armed, but they were strong. The only weapons they used were their beefy arms, *Jake where are you?* It wasn't long before I was thrown in the car and sat in-between two of the largest men I had ever seen, Alec was driving, *where is my angel?*

I was tired and irritable; my walks would usually get out my irritableness before going to sleep with Jake as my personal pillow. I forced myself not to drop to sleep and to do this, I had to constantly twitch, making the two men shudder and stare widely at me.

I wish I knew where they were taking me, to the experimenting labs perhaps, back to Talent School. 1032? Wherever it was, I didn't want to be there. Jake would be realising right now, I'm sure. He would realise that I had not returned and will be on his motorbike aiming his gun at the car's wheels. For a moment, I thought I heard the screeching halt of his bike but it was just my imagination, he wasn't coming, this time I would have to escape myself, just like before. I will use the exit and runaway, Alec cannot keep me caged.

When we got to our destination I sighed with relief, it was the school so my plan of escape could go ahead. I was placed in the Copper block, in the boy's room. I searched for the exit and found it blocked off, all exits were blocked off and Malic and Sophie had gone, but where? I waited and waited for someone to come into my room, it was the middle of the night and there was still no sign of Malic or Sophie, *where are they?* When the door crooked open it was no surprise that I lifted my head in hopeful curiosity. I wish to God, if there is one, that I hadn't, because it was Alec. The same pale-ringed eyes and pasty-skinned Alec, his eyes seemed filled with anger at the sight of me, either anger or… *no, it couldn't be?*

"Where are Sophie and Malic?" I tucked my head back into my knees, I felt like I was ready to burst with tears and it brought me back to that day that I had cried and Alec had held me and kissed me, and it made me gag.

"My guess is they're in the experimenting labs by now," his voice was croakier too.

"Why?" I whispered, he wasn't supposed to hear it.

"They were a part of your little rebellion and so technically, they're criminals…"

"Technically, so are you!" I snapped.

"And you," he whispered. I hadn't noticed how close he had got and now his breath rested unpleasantly in my ear. "We make a great pair, don't you think?"

"No." I'm not a criminal, I'm a rebel, like Jake, we make the perfect pair, not me and Alec, never me and Alec.

"Do you still love me?"

"I never loved you," I spat, "never once did I say, I love you."

"You did, just then."

"Piss off." *I wish he would.*

His hand fell and rested on my hip, I moved away and found myself cornered; funny that I had chosen Chris's bed to sit on, right in the corner. He pulled himself closer and continued to whisper his unpleasant breaths in my ear.

"You do love me." *No I don't, I can't love.* "And I bet you'd do anything for me." *You're delusional Alec, lost in your own world.* "You want to sleep with me."

*No.* "No! I don't."

"Of course you do." What was wrong with him, why was he telling himself these lies? He knew on the day he had told me to stop rebelling that there was no chance of me ever loving him. He was forcing answers into my mouth, they were not my answers and my hand that touched his groin was not my reaction. He had unwillingly pulled my hand to do this and I felt it stiffen at my forced touch.

"And I want to sleep with you, too." He pulled his rolling body over me and I squirmed like a rat in a cage.

"Alec, what's wrong with you?"

"Nothing, I want you, Tanya, Emerald Eyes." *Don't call me that, don't call me Emerald Eyes or Green Eyes. My name is Tanya, Tanya Greyner.*

His body was so heavy on mine I was almost close to fainting, but I didn't for fear of him raping me while I was unconscious, the bastard, the monstrous bastard. He was so hot and sweaty, it was like being in a sauna and not being able to move due to the amount of fat, sweaty people in there. His hands slithered under my top and unhooked my bra, *get off,* he held my breasts in his clammy, pasty hands, *get off*, quickly he pecked me with his dripping mouth, *get off*, I hated it, I hated every moment of it, I hated him, *GET OFF*! I pushed and pulled to get him to let go but his grip was so hard and his body weighed mine down. Fiercely, I pressed my crouched leg against his stomach and kicked, making him topple over onto the floor, slightly winding him.

"You'll pay for that one, bitch," he was about to come near again when I shouted.

"Do it then, go on rape me, you bloody slaughterer, you bloody, rapist slaughterer. I'll call them and tell them exactly what you did and then your head will be chopped off in the experimenting labs."

"And yours, too."

"I'd rather have my body prodded in the experimenting labs than be touched by your slimy hands."

His face came closer to mine and I reached up to slap him, he gripped it and kissed my palm. "We'll see, just wait a few days and you'll come to love me again." *I never loved you, I will never love you.*

I pulled back my hand and rubbed away whatever salvia rested on it. I did not sleep that night in fear of Alec coming back in. I rested on the bed looking up to the ceiling, the boy's room had no windows, unlike the girl's room, and this was probably why Alec had put me in here and not there. I hated him, the slaughtering bastard of a man, *I hate him.*


Two days, it's been two days and already I'm back to my normal routine, almost. Except my normal routine contains my friends and writing, and I haven't been writing and I haven't seen any of my friends, *they're gone, they're all gone.* Only Henry is left and he's not here, he's safe, away. Alec has told me to start another book for them, I won't. I will be put back on the machines again but even more now to make up for when I was not here. Perhaps the plan will still go ahead, of course it will, at least then I won't remember these cruel things, at least the world will still change. I hope to God, if there is one, that it will still change.

I walked down the halls and away from the testing rooms, right where Chris had caught me with Alec that day, every time I thought of Alec touching me I would gag. So much had happened in these halls and hopefully I would soon forget everything, but then technically, I wouldn't. My memories would be replaced by original boarding school memories, so I would still remember the death of Chris, Ruby, Jasper; I would still remember Alec touching me and the feelings I held towards him. I would remember everything horrible, except for those machines. I want to forget everything, all I want to remember is two years ago with my family. I want to remember the world as it once was without those machines or those inhuman experimenting labs. I want to forget the deaths of my friends; I want to forget being with Chris and being touched by Alec, I want to forget it all except one thing, Jake. *I don't want to forget him, but how is that possible? To forget everything and not him, no, none of it is possible, but I wish to God, if there is one, that it was possible, I really do.*

Jake, why hadn't he come? Did he think that I had run away? *Am I not worth it? Where is he? He should be here; he's always here, always here to help me, to save me. Jake, where are you? I need you.*

I was close to Alec's office when Fiona from Silver block came running up to me, also known as Sphene 7.2. It must have been something important for a person from Silver block to talk to a girl from Copper block and by the hurry in her step, I assumed it was.

"Emerald 2.0," I shuddered at that name, it wasn't mine. "There's a boy looking for you."

*A boy, maybe it's Jake, please say it's Jake.* "Who?"

"No one knows who he is, but he says he wanted to find you and..." she came in closer as if she had a secret to tell that no one else was allowed to hear, "...he used your real name."

It had to be Jake. "Where is he? Can you take me to him?"

"Emerald 2.0," Alec stood in the doorway of his room, he smiled politely to Fiona. His mask was propped on his face so perfectly that only I could see through it. "Would you come in here please, I need to speak to you."

*Run Tanya, just like before, run and Jake will find you. He's here, it has to be him.*

"Emerald 2.0, would you please come here? I need to speak with you." *Did he know Jake was here? Was he going to make him leave without me?*

I don't know why, but for some reason I followed his commands and walked slowly into his office. Fiona left with what little information she had, no doubt to gossip; all the girls in the Silver block were notorious for gossiping. Perhaps I walked into Alec's office because I expected Jake to be there, or maybe I thought Alec would return to his normal self and let me leave, let me be happy.

He locked the door after I walked in and went around to his desk, at first I thought he was going to tell me off for something that was his own doing. But he talked casually as if nothing had happened.

"The main programme is soon." *Does he know?*

"Tomorrow."

"No, in five days," he didn't know. But wait, five days, it was supposed to be tomorrow, that's when the plan was going ahead.

"Just got the news a few minutes ago, they changed the dates, five days." He came around the desk and looked into my stunned eyes he did not hesitate to press me against the desk. I could feel his groin stiffen and it scared me, why wouldn't he leave me alone?

"Alec, get off!"

"Just relax to it." No I could never relax to him or his stinging kisses that pierced the skin on my neck. I didn't want this; I wanted this to be Jake. I wanted Jake to force his kiss on to me, because he wouldn't need to force. I wanted him to wrap his arms around me and tug me from side to side, because he wouldn't need to tug. *Jake, please, Jake, please be here, Jake I... I need you, I... I love you, Jake.*

Only I heard the door bash against its hinges, Alec was too busy smothering me. I wriggled harder and harder to get free but his grip was so strong, I had not expected it to be that strong. The door crashed against the wall violently and as if déjà vu had smelt out the scene and come crashing into the room, the scene repeated itself. Alec still clutched me in his grimy hands, only this time, unlike when Chris walked in, it was obvious that I was resisting. He still held me while he talked.

"You're not one of my students."

"And you're not a very good headmaster if this is the way you treat your students," It was Jake, my angel. His eyes flashed over my worried expression, his sweet, powdered, ash-mauve eyes, then they flashed back to Alec. I saw the look that had resembled that of Chris's when he looked at Jake on the motorbike and me on the back clinging to him. This stare was worse though, it was filled with anger, hatred, as if all the deaths that had occurred were because of this man, centred on this one man, holding me, against my will, holding me, *Jake, help me.*

"Let her go!"

"Or what?" Alec pressed me against him harder and smiled.

"Or..." Jake brought out a gun from his leather jacket and pointed it towards Alec. That gun was a piece of magic in that moment, from its sleek black shine to its two-holed muzzle. It was small and it was a piece of a saviour, a piece of Jake. Alec immediately flung me from his grip and stood still, at once I pounded into Jake's free arm and let it curve around me. *Thank God, if there is one, he trusts me; he doesn't think I wanted it, like Chris did. But then again, when I was with Chris, I did want it.*

"Is it really safe to be with this gun-wielding maniac instead of me?" Alec said.

"This gun-wielding maniac," I spat, "is safer than anything else in the world."

With those words piercing through his mind, we left. Jake gripped my hand and we fled to his motorbike and the blackened gates that were the entrance to the school, where Jason was holding it open with no trouble from the limp guards flopped on the floor. On seeing us, he got in his car and drove off, leaving us to drive away on our own. It was strange but we had no disturbances from the authorities, we escaped with relative ease.

Jake stopped his motorbike at a park where a water fountain trickled the sun's silver light off its spouting ornaments and where the leaves fell crisply from the trees and joined the other foliage that rested on the ground. He dismounted and sat on a bench near the water fountain, looking only at the water's clear reflection. I felt horrible, *he must hate me now, I hate me.* I walked towards him and stopped halfway.

"I'm sorry," tears trickled down my face like the silver water off every ornament. He looked up and I looked down, I couldn't bear to look at him, *he must hate me.* Yet he got up and folded his arms around me, resting his chin on my head.

"Did he hurt you?" His voice was so soft, so comforting and instantly I was back to falling asleep at the sound of it.

"I'm fine, I'm sorry."

"Why? you didn't do anything wrong," his chin was so perfectly placed on my head, as if there was a weak spot on it that he could always find.

We stayed in the park for a while and talked. Soon enough, I fell asleep and woke up back in the haven with his body curled around me. I don't know how he got me back to the haven, but I'm glad he did and I'm glad he kept me in his room and didn't put me back in mine. *I love you, Jake, I just wish I could tell you, I wish I could say it, 'I love you, Jake.'*

At first, I rested in his arms, back to the way things were, safe, with Jake. Thank God, if there is one, that I'm not with Alec in that hell school anymore. I didn't remember what Alec had told me at first, I was too swayed by Jake and only until he mentioned it, did I remember.

"Morning," he smiled, "Tanya."

I didn't reply but edged closer to his body and felt up his chest, he was still smiling while I gently folded his shirt up and pressed my fingers into the crevasses of his slim six-pack. He looked up and rested his head against the wall, making a piece of paper crumble as his spiked hair ruffled it.

"Everything will be better after today,"

It didn't hit me at first; I was still in my world where everyone knew what I knew and where they could easily read my mind, especially Jake.

"How?" As if this world could ever really be better.

"It's the big programme today, don't you remember?" He laughed gently and leaned over me stretching his arm out to reach the alarm clock, it read 11:50, we had slept in late, then again, we had gotten in pretty late.

"In ten minutes, in fact, I think I'll have a shower." He got up and took off his t-shirt with me gladly watching, then he turned to me and couldn't help but slip his hand to my cheek.

"Well, I don't think anyone will mind if we sleep in and wake up in the new world together," he pressed his cool lips on my forehead, then nuzzled my neck.

I laughed. "We've already slept in... Wait, ten minutes, today!" I rose up and looked at him with my shocked expression, he was so calm and I couldn't believe it.

"Yeah, Tanya, what's wrong?"

"It's not today," I shouted.

"What?"

I rushed up and took my jacket from the desk; Jake was still topless and shocked. "The programme, it's changed."

"What?" I looked at the clock; it now read 11:55.

"It's changed. Alec said it's changed to five days away, so it should be four days away now."

His eyes widened.

"The others don't know, we have to warn them, quick." Jake rushed, still topless, through the halls and I followed. If we didn't get there in time then everything would be ruined. We would have to wait another two years to start the plan again; but then again, another two years with Jake wouldn't be that bad, but another two years of countless murders would be bad. We ran as fast as we could, who knew how long we were taking, it felt like years and as I ran, the world devoured me in its time and I saw how the world used to be, it was more peaceful than this world, a better world, that was why we were running, to revisit that world, to bring it back. And if we didn't make it in time, none of it would become true, the dream that was once so real was turning to ash, it was being slaughtered, just like the people in the experimenting labs. We have to run, because if we don't, this world will never get a chance to go back to the way it was, and the way it was before was perfect. New technology like this hadn't helped us, it had made it worse. The machines had been offered as a peace offering to any countries that were at war and they took them, peace lasted for three weeks and then they fought over the machines, wanting more and more. They tried to make their own and soon enough they had discovered how to do it all and followed Britain by creating experimenting labs, causing more war. Every country pretended that the labs were wholesome places where simple experiments were done and people were well looked after. They weren't just murderers they were liars, murdering liars.

I stumbled over one foot and fell, Jake was a few steps ahead of me and he quickly jolted back and helped me by gripping the crook of my elbow and pressing his hand against the bone of my back. Even now, when we were in danger, I was melting at his cool touch, he was still topless and had not bothered to bring anything with him to put on as we ran. I wondered why he was helping me and why he wasn't just running ahead to tell them, as he was obviously much faster than me.

"Come on," he urged, not in a commanding voice but in a gruff voice that made the caramel wave out and ring in my ears.

I stumbled up just as I had fell down, with his help, and he pulled me by the hand to the next hallway and down to where the machines were kept. I couldn't be sure but I think there was about a minute before Taroff would start the programme. Jake was faster than me and almost dragging me along, and I huffed breathlessly as he pulled me, panting like a dying wolf, or worse. I picked up my pace as I remembered why we were doing this, for the new type of world we would create, free of those hideous machines. I imagined it all, somewhat like the top of the building Jake had showed me on his birthday. With the light pouring golden over the town's darkened buildings and making each window gleam with a sort of colour that added hope to the world. I could see the world without machines as orange, yellow, topaz, gold and not red, the world we were in was already red. Painted with the lives of so many people and stained with their sweat and blood, I almost imagined the slaughterers as vampires, hungry for blood and we would rid the world of these vampires by flashing a golden ray to the top of the world and back. That's why I ran, if I didn't run, I would never get to see the world wrapped in golden light; even if people didn't remember how it used to be ,it doesn't matter. Even though they will not realise how amazing the world is, it won't matter. Sure, they'll try to create machines again, but that's why people like Jake are here, and me.

We got to the silver sliding doors and they were locked. Why in God's name, if there is one, did they lock it? Jake fiercely threw his fists to the door and shouted; I knew he, too, thought that the world would be just as beautiful as that setting sun that he showed me.

"God damn it," if there is one, "open up," he shouted.

The doors burst open with an exhausting breath and we fumbled in and searched the room. Taroff and Henry were about to do whatever they thought was necessary. Jason was in the corner looking at us puzzled, and Pete was in the other corner also looking just as puzzled.

"Don't do it!" Jake cried.

"What?" Jason came over and pushed gently against Jake's head, "What the hell is wrong with you?"

"They changed the date of the programme," I said. "It should be four days from now, if you do it now it will all be ruined."

Taroff's eyes widened, please tell me he hasn't done it, please don't let it be too late.

"Get the other countries on the phone, NOW!" he blazed. "Jason, phone America, Pete, France, I'll phone Japan, tell them to alert all the other countries immediately, if they don't already know."

"Countries?" I puzzled, my breath still wheezy and hoarse.

"I told you," Jake started, his voice rippling through my ears, I swayed and almost fell over at the sound of his voice and he caught my arm and helped me up. "There are rebels just like us all over the world, in every country, they're all following the same plan, if they didn't it wouldn't work."

"Arigato," Taroff placed the phone in his pocket and sighed. The others finished speaking to France and America too and did the same. "They know, apparently they all know, they're going to double check and phone up everyone just to make sure. Goddamn it, that was so close, four days then, in four days, we can wait that long, right?" It didn't seem like a question; though the question mark hovered over it, I could not see it as a question, neither real nor rhetorical. It was like Taroff was thinking whether he could wait or not, I could never imagine what he had seen, the deaths he had been through, this plan was his life and if it didn't succeed then he would die, naturally or not.

"How did you know?" Henry perched on the edge of his chair and looked towards me. He looked older, more mature and we had not been here for that long, *have we?* I couldn't remember.

"Alec," was all I said, though I would have loved to add, 'Alec, the bastard, monstrous, slaughtering, two-faced murdering liar.' Yes, I would have loved to add that, but I didn't.

"Right, I know we're all a bit panicky but everything is fine now. We go ahead with the plan in four days. Taroff, make sure you've got all the information right, and Tanya," Jason stared at me with a stern face that turned bright with a smile.

156

"Thank you." He didn't bother saying thank you to his brother. Maybe because it was his brother and he didn't think he needed to or maybe because he knew, the slight twinkle in his eye made me realise that it was the second one.

"And you?" he turned to Jake, his bare chest glistening from the ominous orange lights, his body sparkling with sweat from our run. "For God's sake, go put a shirt on or something, God only knows what you were doing before you came here." It made me laugh as Jake scowled at his brother; in a way, Jason's rudeness was always comforting. They said the word 'God' as if he really was real and watching over them, it made me think. The way they said it made him seem real even to me; how could people who had lost almost everything believe in him? It seemed impossible.

"That was close," Jake sat down on the bed, then flopped his head backwards to the pillow, even though his t-shirt was right beside him, he didn't put it on.

"Are you going to have a shower now?"

"I don't know, I certainly am sweatier now," he certainly was and the moisture clung to him as if it, too, could not resist being close to him.

"Lovely," I said. He laughed at this little remark, though it wasn't really a remark, I was just stating a fact, he really was lovely, everything about him was lovely.

I watched him close his eyes and sigh outwards as if he was controlling himself from leaping up and pressing me against him. In a way, I wanted that and in a way, I didn't, because if he did that he wouldn't be Jake anymore, he'd be like Chris or Alec, but then again, at least for a while, I would...

"Jake?" He was sleeping, I had never seen him sleeping before, I had always fallen asleep first. He was even more like an angel when he slept; his breath circled his lips. If only I deserved those lips, those electric lips. I was surprised he was so tired, even though we stayed out quite late, we had had a good few hours of sleep. Maybe during those two long days I wasn't here he didn't

157

sleep at all? There were certainly shadows under his eyes, his beautiful ash-mauve eyes.

I realised that, like him, I was hot and frustrated after the sprint to the machines; funny, I never thought I would sprint to those machines, until today. Carefully, I tiptoed past him and walked into the shower room, I kept the door unlocked and even thought about opening it slightly. But then, he would wake up and I didn't want to wake an angel from his slumber. I looked at the door's lock and grazed a finger over it, in a way I was tempting him and I shouldn't have been.

Just as quietly as I had tiptoed, I undressed and let the water from the shower trickle off me, my hair had grown a bit longer since I had ran away and I didn't like it too long. After the shower, I rooted through the drawers under the sink and found a pair of scissors. Carefully, I angled them towards my hair and cut. I placed the hair in the bin that rested next to the sink and went back into the shower to wash away any hair that stuck to my body. With the towel clinging to me, I watched my reflection in the mirror, my hair was fine, not professionally cut and it was dripping wet, but it was fine.

With my towel still clinging to my wet body, I peered through to the room where Jake was still sleeping. His slow sighs as mesmerising as his voice. I shuffled over to him quietly; half hoping to trip and wake him up so that he'd see I was half bare. My fingers were still wet and slowly I stroked down from his spiked up hair to his jaw line, he was even more beautiful when he slept. I leant in and kissed his forehead, it was like he was kissing me back, electric still flowed through my veins.

"Sweet dreams, my angel."


We were all counting down the days, *three days left*. It would be done at the same time and everything was set ready. Taroff was frequently watching out for new changes and constantly hacked into important databases and other things I would never in my life have been able to reach on a computer, or in any other way. Everyone was on edge, except me and Jake. Hearing the news first hand seemed to make us resistant to any paranoia or fear. We floated lightly through the halls when we were apart and together, and anyone who saw us would always seem to notice something apparently 'different' about us, especially Jason with Jake. I still slept in Jake's room, it was peaceful there, all we did was sleep, all we ever did was sleep, the occasional kiss here and there but mostly, he just liked to hold me and I liked to be held. It was as if he was somehow afraid to hurt me, as if going any further would strain things and would make him seem beastly and aggressive, he was protective of me. Chris was protective, but only because he knew if something happened, I could no longer be there for him, to talk to him, to help him, to pleasure him. Alec was protective, but only because he wanted me to be his and his alone. However, Jake was protective because, he didn't want anything to hurt me, not because he's possessive like Alec or thinks that's how it should be, like Chris, *no, it's because he wants to protect me, care for me and love me, and he does and I love him, too, I just can't say it, not yet anyway, not yet.*

# Chapter 8

I strolled down the hall with my constant smile framing my face. Everything would be perfect soon, back to the way things used to be and I would be with Jake, the most perfect thing of all.

Jason rushed past me, almost knocking me over in his hurry. At first he didn't notice me.

"Tanya!"

I turned around and regained my balance, so it was me he was rushing around looking for.

"Yes?" I said while my hand rested on my forehead.

"He's been taken."

"Who?" No! *God, if there is one, no! Is it Jake, Jake is taken?* The world started to spin around me and I fell to the floor. *He cannot be taken, he's my saviour, my hero, my rebel, my angel, Jake, no!*

"Tanya," Jason rushed to my side and propped me against the wall. "It's fine, everything will be fine."

"No, no it won't, they've taken him."

"I know, but we might be able to get him back before..."

"Before? No, no we have to get him back. If he dies, then I..."

"Tanya, it will be fine, we're getting everyone in the meeting room now to discuss quickly, then we'll be off."

"It won't be fine," I panicked, "we have to go now, we have to go and save Jake now."

"Jake?" His puzzled expression calmed. "Jake's fine, he's here. It's Henry, Henry's the one who's been taken."

"Henry? My head spun around once more and suddenly I saw Henry standing in the experimenting labs, in the same room Chris was in, a man came from behind him with an axe and with each chop he made on Henry's head, I grew more distant from the scene and back to reality. **Chop**. Blood trickled down his neck. **Chop**. I heard the cracking sounds of Henry's spine. **Chop**. The man behind him laughed. **Chop**. Henry fell. **Chop**. I heard Jason's voice.

"Tanya, Tanya."

"Jason," my eyes opened, I had fainted but not for long, "Where is Jake?"

"In the meeting room with the others,"

I swooped up and ran faster than Jason had ran before, I needed to see him and confirm that he was here and that it was Henry in danger. I needed him to hold me and tell me that everything was alright. I couldn't let Henry go through the hell that was the experimenting labs like almost all my other friends, he had to be safe, he had to survive, I needed a friend from the past beside me.

The doors opened with a loud clatter and I stood in the centre of the doorway, shocked and still.

"Tanya," Jake pounced from his seat and held me, he could see that I was shocked, he rested his hand against the back of my head. His t-shirt became stained with my salty tears. I was so glad it wasn't him taken, but I still needed Henry back, I needed a friend from the past and he was the only one left standing.

"It's ok, Tanya, it's fine," he soothed.

"We have to get him back, it can't happen again, I can't lose another friend, not another."

Jason bounded through the doors, almost making as much as a dramatic entrance as I had. Jake led me to a seat and Jason took to the front of the room.

"Can we get him back?"

Taroff was the one to answer. "If we're seen taking him, it might cause suspicion. However, if they find him missing, then they will think nothing of it."

"Dumb ass slaughterers," Jason stammered. "So, we can't be seen, ay? Well then, not too many people. How do we get in?"

"Well…"

"There's a secret passage under the sewers. I've been there before. I can take you there if you want," I said.

"Taroff, your way in is?"

"Through the doors where we would be seen by multiple security cameras."

"Sounds like we're going with your idea, Tanya. Techs, what about security cameras?"

He smiled, it was the first time I had seen him smile. "Hook this into one of them and I will be able to cover them over for a while with an old recording of the place for each one, just for a while, though."

"What is it?" Jake searched the small device which was now rolling in Taroff's hand.

"It doesn't matter, just connect it to one security camera and it will be done."

"They're so small these days, though, how will we connect it, see it even?" I asked.

"I can tell you when you're near a security camera and will give you a device to see it, all you have to do is place it over it. Make sure you do it close to where you're going in and out so that you can take it as soon as."

"So who goes?" Jason also smiled as if the danger was nothing but fun. "Tanya, obviously, as she knows the way in and…"

"I'll go," Taroff stood up.

"We need you to operate the controls from here, keep an eye out on things, just leave it." Taroff nodded.

"It's a lifted-up floorboard to get in so it's not huge."

"No Pete or me then, guess it's just you two, alright with that, Jake?"

"Yeah," he breathed, he seemed scared, "that's fine," but I didn't know why.

"Take these ear pieces," Taroff slid them across the table. They were smaller than the tip of my forefinger and were sticky so they could be placed just inside the rim of our ear. "And these," he slid a pair of chunky, black sunglasses over the table and Jake put them on, he looked amazingly cool in them, but it made me unnerved when I couldn't see his eyes, so I pulled them down so they could rest on his nose, his eyes were sad and frightened, why?

"Those will help you see the cameras, the cameras will basically be dots but they will flash red and the glasses will focus on them, got it?"

"Got it," his voice sounded sombre too.


We didn't take the motorbike, though I longed to rest my head against his cool leather jacket and wrap my hands around his warm chest. We went to Thirty-Four Street, and to the door with 'Davis was 'ere', to Thirty-Eight Street, into the street and down the grate, we followed the water and passed the first two ladders, and stopped at the third.

"Up here." I looked up the ladder, it seemed larger than it should have been, as if we would climb up it forever and get nowhere, then fall.

"Right, wait here, I'll be back soon."

"What?"

"You heard me," his voice was suddenly sharp and dull.

"I'm coming in with you."

"It will be easier if you don't."

"Jake, I've been here before…"

"So have I!" His voice was stern, and then I finally realised why he had been so sad, frightened and sombre before. He was afraid I would get hurt, caught, lost or worse.

"I mean here and not being experimented on," he twitched and looked away from me, what I said must have stung.

"Stay here, Tanya." He took one step up the ladder and started to pull himself up, I pulled on the back of his cool leather jacket.

"Jake, I'm coming in with you," he dropped down to face me and his eyes dug into mine. Those beautiful eyes that had always swayed me, now scared me.

"Tanya, please, I don't want to lose you again."

"You never lost me."

He looked away then touched a hand to my face without looking in my eyes. He pulled my head to the crook of his neck so I could rest against it. His breath fell on my hair, mangled from the constant running.

"You were lost, because every second that you weren't cradled in my arms, I felt ill. I couldn't breathe, I couldn't sleep. At first, Jason told me to wait, he said you'd come back, in under an hour I was panicking. I waited and then I searched, every second you weren't next to me, near me, you were lost and I was lost without you, Tanya, I don't think I can live without you anymore. I couldn't imagine going to sleep without your whispering breath resting on my pillow; I think I've fallen in love with you, Tanya, and I shouldn't have." *He still hasn't said 'I love you' though and I haven't said it either, it's as if we both can't bear to say it, as if it hurts.*

"I shouldn't be able to love anyone. Ever since my parents died and I was taken away, I swore I would only love Jason as a brother should love a brother, but when I saw you in the library, something changed and that kiss..." he stroked his own lips and kept his fingers placed on the edge of his mouth, "...it felt... electric."

"Electric," I breathed.

"It's not like I haven't seen girls before, interacted with them, kissed them even, but... you were different, somehow the same, but different." He took away his fingers from his hands and held me tighter.

I reached out for the bar but he held my hand.

"Tanya, please," his eyes were softer now, they seemed delicate and jewel like, I wanted to test to see if they were real jewels.

"Jake, I promise that I will always be with you. I... couldn't live without you either, please let me go, I need to see for myself."

He nodded, but it was a very slow, small nod. Jake put on his glasses so that he would see the hidden security cameras, though I knew he was putting them on to cover his saddened eyes.

He helped me out of the lifted tile and looked around to search for cameras.

"Taroff, we're in," he said, holding onto his ear, most likely pressing down on the small earpiece Taroff had given us.

"Right, do you see a camera?" Taroff's voice echoed through my ear and Jake's.

I couldn't see what it looked like through Jake's glasses, but in my mind it centred on a small red dot on the wall and then the dot became surrounded and highlighted by surrounding red squares, with writing crossing the top of the glasses.

"Right, then, place it over the camera," Jake did as commanded. "From this, I should also be able to see where Henry is being kept and can guide you there."

It took a matter of seconds for Taroff to get all the essential information needed.

"Ok, go down the hall and to the right there's a staircase. Go up it then stop at the edge of the corner, there's a woman coming down the hall in the opposite direction, wait till I give you the ok."

We followed his directions and stopped at the edge of the corner.

"Alright, she's gone into a room. Go down the hall and when you get to the end, go left then up at the first crossing."

"Are we in an experimenting lab or on a road?" Jake whispered.

"Just do it, Jake." We did.

"Ok, then, go down the left and stop after three doors, at the fourth." I could imagine Taroff, Pete and Jason watching us run along the corridors via the hacked-into cameras, feeling just as tense as we were.

"He's in there," Jake reached for the button to open the door but it failed.

"There's a touch screen lock on it," Jake said while holding down his ear.

"You got the metal plaster I gave you."

"Yeah,"

"Good, they're not plasters. Place it on the touch screen, then when you press the button, the door should open." He did, and it did.

We hurried into the room and searched from corner to corner for Henry; he was slumped on a chair against the back wall hooked up to a machine neither of us had ever seen. One spider-like metal helmet was attached to the top of his forehead and he was strapped into the chair.

"How do we get him out?" I asked.

"I've got more of those plaster things." He placed one on each brace that surrounded the legs and arms; it looked like an electric chair of some sort.

The plasters worked and carefully Jake pulled away the helmet and caught Henry as he flopped, he was knocked out.

"Wow, those plasters do everything."

"Better pick them up, don't want to leave evidence, and the one on the touch screen near the door."

"Right." I followed his caramel command and soon enough we were listening to Taroff again giving us the ok.

As we ran past a room, something caught my eye, it was a room that had a clear window to see into it. The room on the inside was padded and small with a figure curled up in the corner. It was Malic.

"Wait, Jake!"

"What?" He turned around and I placed my hand in the pocket he had got the plasters out of, there was one left.

"What are you doing?" He whispered, puzzled by my sudden unlocking of the door.

"It's Malic."

"Malic?"

"A friend."

"Tanya, we can't go around searching for all of your friends and taking them away, they'll get suspicious, they'll know something is wrong."

"It's not all of my friends, it's just Malic and he's coming with us." Malic rose his head to the sound of the door unlocking.

Jake pressed his finger to his ear. "Taroff, is it ok to take one more, will it raise too much suspicion?"

"It's too late now, just hurry and take him, a man is about to come around the corner, hurry, and Jake, don't get caught."

"Tanya, hurry, there's a man coming."

"Malic, Malic, it's us, come on, we're here to get you."

"Leave," he whispered. "They'll get you, run, just go."

"Tanya!"

"Malic, please, come, quick," he placed his head back in his hands and swayed from side to side. I pulled him and with little resistance he got up, I had to drag him, but he came.

We just made it before the man had slipped around the corner, but we made it, we made it back to the tile and took off the equipment from the security camera, then we went down, and away from the hell that was the experimenting labs; it was always the experimenting labs.


Two sleeps left and then the plan would go ahead. Taroff was constantly edgy and now and then he would check on Henry. The two had bonded pretty well and now he was like a younger brother to him. Henry was still sleeping and Malic was still in shock. It was only until Henry woke up that Malic started to become fine again, as if Henry waking up was an awakening for Malic at the same time. Malic didn't bother to explore like Henry and Chris had done when they first got here, instead he followed Henry around from room to room, reminiscing about the old days. In a way, you could tell that this annoyed Henry, like us, he didn't want things to be like they were in the 'old days', but he tolerated it as he suspected that Malic was just scared and this was his way of seeking comfort.

When Henry recovered fully, he spent more time with Taroff working on whatever needed to be worked on. Malic began to cling to me then, and Henry recovered in less than a few hours so it wasn't long before I had a Malic attached to me.

"So, where is this exactly?"

"You know the old petrol station we used to pass on the way to the Rain dance club?" I sighed; he had been asking a lot of questions.

"Yeah."

"Well, it's across from there, underground."

"Underground, huh?" We reached the room where Henry and Taroff were working on something I didn't even want to try and understand.

With Malic constantly hanging around me, Jake didn't seem to come near me often; I suspected that he was jealous, not that he would ever admit to being jealous.

"Hey, Henry," Malic beamed, suddenly all of his shock dissolved.

"Hey," he didn't look up from the work him and Taroff were doing. They seemed to be calculating something as they had holographic calculators coming from a small square on the table, and papers with scratchy writing on them; they both had terrible handwriting. Taroff didn't seem to like Malic very much, the looks that he cast on him were neither evil nor friendly and when he did look at him, he glanced over him as if anything but him was interesting.

"So, umm... what are you up to?" Malic smiled, not yet hurt by the unwelcomed greetings.

"Calculating how much power it would take to destroy the closest experimenting labs, and how big the machine would need to be." Henry carried on scribbling as he spoke and Taroff briefly looked up to frown at Malic, probably expecting him to know what they were doing straight away.

"Did Jason tell you to do that?" I asked.

"No," Taroff laughed, "but we figured it might be useful since we will need to take them down afterwards, not to mention move the people."

Jason and Jake walked through the doors and as Jake saw that Malic wasn't pursuing me, he came closer and shaped his arm to fit my waist.

"Take who down, what are you doing?" Malic questioned.

"We're getting rid of the knowledge machines, Malic, and returning things back to the way they should be," Jake smiled as he heard the admiration in my voice. I wanted this almost more than anything else in the world, except for one thing that is.

"What? But, how? Why?"

We only answered the third question, everyone was tired of explaining the plan, we just wanted to get it done.

"Why?" I laughed. "Why? Because they're the reason the world is a mess, that's why."

"What are you talking about, the world is fine."

"Are you insane?" Henry launched. "The world is far from fine, you were in those experimenting labs, you must have seen what went on, what goes on. What the hell is wrong with you, Malic? Don't you want things to be normal, back to the forgotten ways, the perfect ways people can't remember?"

"Stupid tales of everyone not being separated, no Talent Schools and experimenting labs, all lies and fairy tales."

"They're not make believe," Jake brawled; his face was full of anger and so was mine. "It's true, the way things used to be. Good, perfect, no pointless murders for experiments, no idiots who take people on the edge of life to experiment and kill them even more." I looked up to Jake, his jaw clenched as well as his balled-up fist, I knew that he was thinking of his parents and what the slaughterers had done to them.

"So what?" Malic spat. "You're going to change the world, ha, it's useless, you can't get rid of those machines and why would you? They help people, they give everyone opportunities. They help dumb people get an education, a good job, they help people with natural talent get fame, fortune."

"Lies," I spat back. "No one knows we're the ones with talent, no one knows we're the ones making those pictures, stories, writing those songs."

"My voice is heard on every CD I sing for."

Henry rolled off his chair to stand and lurched closer to Malic, "and what about in a few years, when they decide to take away your voice and just keep the music, how about then? Will you be happy then?"

"We're famous, Henry, me, you and Tanya, our songs are out there, your books, Tanya…"

"And you think that's good? You think people know there mine? NO, they don't."

"If things go back to the way they're supposed to, then we won't have a chance to get our books and songs, music and artwork out at this age."

"We will, we'll just have to try harder, we'll earn it."

"You want to have to work harder?" he pinched his eyes together and glared through them.

"You wouldn't know a day's work if it hit you in the face," Jake whispered, but so everyone could hear it.

"You're all crazy; I'm getting out of here." Malic ran through the door and down the halls. That was the last time I saw Malic.

"Jason," Jake called.

"Yeah, I know," with that, Jason pursued Malic in the direction he had run.

"Is he going to catch him and bring him back?" I sounded so sweet and innocent but Jake did not return my innocence, he just looked down with a stare that was neither worried nor stern, and yet it scared me.

"Jake, he'll bring him back, won't he?"

He shook his head slowly. "If he tries to escape and if he doesn't agree with what we're doing, he could…" he left it at that.

"No," I gasped. "No, you can't kill him, Henry, they'll…" but Henry was facing away, his mind had already made its decision. He had already moved on from how things were, Malic was nothing to him anymore, but even if Malic hadn't always been one of the best friends I had ever had, I still couldn't let him die, I couldn't let another friend die.

I ran, just as Malic had ran and Jason had ran, I ran. As I turned the corner of the hall, Jason was there, his back turned away from me.

"Jason, don't…" but it was already too late, as I edged closer I could see Malic's listless body smothering the floor, one hole shot perfectly in the back of his head. Jason put the safety lock back on his gun and hid it back in his pocket. He didn't turn around to face

171

me, what could he say, what could he do? He had already killed him and though in a way Malic should have been was nothing to me, I still wished Jason hadn't killed him. Malic was a cruel, idiotic boy who only wanted the world to stay as it was for his own selfish reasons, too stubborn to see that if he stepped outside into the world once more, it would devour him and spit him back into the experimenting labs, fool. But he was a fool I had known; out of all the fools I had known, I would have never imagined mourning his death the most, but I did. His death finally made me realise the strength of the world, of each brutal individual. This world was a cruel, murdering place and even the heroes, even the angels, were cruel, murderous monsters. His death made so many memories flourish back, good memories and bad. I saw my family again, happy, playing, arguing, dead, but they weren't dead; I knew they weren't dead, this was a false memory. I saw each death of my friends, Chris, Jasper; I heard the screams and swelling of Ruby, those screams rotted my brain and turned memories into nightmares. My mind ached and I had to lean against the wall and hold it to balance myself, hoping this would make the pain go away, it didn't.

"Tanya!" Jason reached out his hand and I slapped it away and fell as I did so.

The world was spinning and suddenly Malic's body twitched and got up. I pressed my fingers to the back of my neck and it was me who had been shot, me with the perfect hole in the back of my neck. Malic laughed, no, he cackled. "You're all crazy; I'm getting out of here," then he ran and everything was gone, everyone was gone. I was left in a black nothingness where only Malic's last words echoed.

"You're all crazy."

"You're all crazy."

"I'm getting out of here."

"I'm getting out of here."

"You're all crazy."

"I'm getting out of here."

"I'm getting out of here."

"I'm getting out of here."


"Tanya, Tanya!"

When I opened my eyes, I was cradled in Jake's arms with Henry and Jason hovering over me. It looked like I hadn't been out for that long. At first, I was happy to see Jake but then I looked over to where Malic should have been and he wasn't there.

"Where's Malic?"

"Gone," Jake soothed stroking my hair from the back to the front.

"Gone?"

"Buried," Henry said; he said it with such ease, not a pang of regret in his voice.

My eyes widened greatly and I shuffled away from Jake's grip, clawing at the floor as I did so. His eyes were still soothing and gentle, but I couldn't look at them, it hurt.

"Tanya, it's ok," his hand went to touch me but like I had with Jason's, I swatted it away.

"Don't touch me," I screamed. "You're just like them."

"What?" His gentle eyes slowly turned into a scowl as he realised who I was talking about.

"You murder people, slaughter them, just like them."

He stood up and backed away from me, disgusted as if I was filth, smut. "I am nothing like them. Do you understand that? I am nothing like them, do I harbour bodies to experiment on?"

"You may as well," I shouted, "you kill people like they're nothing, then what am I, Jake? Nothing."

"Tanya," he tried to reach out again and I moved back.

"I said, don't touch me." This time I ran because I was scared, not scared of Malic being killed, but scared of everything, this world was a scary place.

I ended up running to one of the passages that lead outside. I should have been more cautious about wandering outside again, but I didn't think that Alec would be back any time soon and I wasn't afraid of anyone else in the outside world. I wasn't going to walk far, just far enough to think of what I wanted to do, if I wanted to stay. The haven wasn't a particularly bad place, but I had never seen them kill anyone that was innocent, especially my friend, and it scared me. What if I had wandered into the haven without an invitation one day, would I have been shot, too?

The image of Malic's blank expression played in my mind over and over again. The hole in his head filled my empty mind instead of emptying his.

I came to an empty bench just outside an abandoned car wash and sat down. The picture of Malic floated back to my mind; suddenly I could feel myself in his position again, dead. But this time I was the one who got up and Jason, Jake, Henry, Pete and Taroff were running to me, no they were running at me, guns at the ready, their eyes glazed over black. I ran, the bullet fell from my head and shot back to Henry, he fell too, then the bullet jumped from his head and did the same to Taroff and then Pete and then Jason, everyone but Jake. Jake stopped running and I found myself frozen and facing him, the bullet hole in my head gone and his glazed black eyes back to their normal ash-mauve. He smiled and dropped his gun. It toppled to the floor and skidded beside my feet.

*Tanya*, he went out to touch me but I backed away, *Tanya, please.*

Then his face was no longer his, it was Alec's, then Chris's and then it was his again and the gun shook on the floor, then it quivered in the air and then in my hand. Before I could tell my hand to stop, it had already acted and Jake was dead on the floor, a bullet hole in his head, just like the others. A small dot of blood spread from his head to the floor, it grew larger and larger then spread to me, and the ceiling, and the walls, and the floor started to rain blood.

*Jake*

My eyes opened and I jolted from the bench upwards, my breath quivered just as the gun had quivered in my dream's hand. I looked up to the sky and realised it was raining, I was soaked. My dream was so vivid and so fuzzy, it scared me even more and made me realise I wasn't going to sleep out here in the rain all night, so I went back to the haven.

# Chapter 9

That was the first night, besides when I was back in Talent School, that I stayed in my room. I locked the door and had a shower with the door closed and locked. I didn't sleep that night and I suspected that Jake didn't either, good, I didn't want him to.

That day, I mostly stayed in my room, only venturing out to get food from the kitchen. The big programme was tomorrow and yet all I could think about was the deaths of my friends. I wanted to forget it all, I wanted to forget everything that had happened, and though I knew if I was held by Jake's arms I would be calmer and the thoughts would fade away, I knew they would just return when he let me go.

At six o'clock my stomach began to grumble far too much and the aching pain wasn't something I liked to ignore, so I rushed to the kitchen area hoping to get in and out with something to eat quickly. The door to the kitchen was already open and someone was rummaging through the fridge, it was Jake and without looking at me he pulled out a can of pop, he pretended not to notice me at first, but I knew he did.

I ignored him and went to the cupboard in search of food and a glass; I found a cereal bar, a bread roll and an carton of orange juice, but no glass. Trying to seem calm, I pulled open each metal cupboard in search of a glass. Looking up and down and finding none, I cursed in my head, I didn't want to be near Jake for too long. He went to the corner of the room and opened the cupboard that was fixed into the wall; he took a quick glance at me then walked over and placed a glass by my hand, brushing it gently. He walked slower than he needed to to the door and sighed.

"Tanya." Silence. "I'm sorry, really I am."

More silence.

"Do you want to sleep in my room tonight?"

"Do you want me to sleep in your room?" The question was not as soft as it had previously been, it was sharp and I knew without turning that it hit home.

"Always," it sounded like a whimper, a begging and a gentle whisper all in one.


I decided not to eat after he left; I took the glass of orange back to my room and slowly sipped it. When it was all gone, I couldn't help but cry. The clock on my wall flashed eight, in sixteen hours the world would be different, better and I didn't want to go into a new beginning with me being mad at Jake or the other way around. I hesitantly wandered to Jake's door; the door that had always been open was now closed. I reached out to touch the cold metal handle and couldn't seem to open it, I just stroked it gently as if this was as close as I was ever going to get to Jake.

"Were you going to go in?" I span around fiercely to meet his eyes, those sweet, powdered, ash-mauve eyes.

"I…" I collapsed on the floor and broke down into tears, "I'm so sorry."

He immediately jolted down to me and spread his arms across and around me, bringing me closer to his chest and making me wrap my arms around him to the inside of his leather jacket.

"I'm sorry," I sniffed, like the pathetic girl I saw myself as. "You must hate me, I'm sorry, I am so, so sorry."

He didn't reply but swept me up in his arms and brought me into his room. Carefully, he placed me on the bed and watched me look up with watered eyes. He stroked from my cheek to my jaw and took my chin in his thumb and finger. He sat on the edge of the bed and leaned over, coming closer to my face. "Tanya," his breath swept my lips and created an electric current that pulsed through my body and down. He kissed my chin then up to meet my lips, curling them upwards with an electric force that continually swept through my entire bodies, sending hot shivers down my spine. As he retracted, I kept my eyes closed, I didn't want him to see that my eyes were still full of tears, though I was sure he knew as he flicked one off my cheek.

"*I love you.*" At first, these words were a dream, a beautiful dream that I would soon wake up from. I was still in Talent School and the library, the alleyway, the park and everything to do with Jake and changing the world was just a dream, a beautiful swaying dream and I wanted to stay in a dream like that forever.

"Tanya, *I love you,*" he leant in close and whispered in my ear, his caramel voice swaying me. "Please, never leave me, *I love you.*" No matter how many times he said those words, I couldn't get over the shock that followed them, he loved me and he had said it. I wish I could say it, I want to say it, but I haven't said it, not yet, not yet.

He looked up to see my eyes open, tears still trickling down them, but for a different reason. He was smiling, his sweet, shining smile. I remember that night ending with him kissing me on the forehead and his arms encasing me once more, my memories floated away but I was sure they would soon return.


We woke up at half past nine and hurried to the rooms where the chairs and the main controls for the plan where kept. Everyone was already in there, Jason, Pete, Taroff and Henry. They were double checking everything and making sure everything was secure. It was almost time, after today the world would be different, everything would be perfect and I would remember this great accomplishment, I would remember everything. The change of the world, being held by Jake, floating away to the moon on his bike, meeting him, the deaths of my friends, Alec, Talent School. 1032, I would remember it all.

We sat in silence for an hour, anxious and scared of what the future had in store for us; whatever it was, we were ready. We had planned for failure and we had planned for the opposite, either way we were ready. Yet something from inside me nagged at my minds swirling thoughts, the world tumbled down into my mind and made my brain ache. *Will it be like this forever? Will I constantly think of the past, the horrible past, forever? I don't want to, I want*

178

*those bad memories to go away and I only want the good ones here.*

"Fifteen minutes," Taroff said. Each one of us tensed, something that hadn't been possible for so long was about to happen, the world was about to change, it had to change.

"Check everything again and make sure everything's perfect, the programme, the information, the ending, the connection, everything." Taroff did as Jason commanded and typed faster than I had ever seen him or anyone type. We all tightened our grip, if something was wrong, just one little thing, everything would be ruined.

"Everything is perfect, five minutes."

"Right, sit tight," Jason nodded.

"Four minutes."

Taroff would start when two minutes were remaining, then everything would be different, everything. This world would no longer remember the way things were, only the countless amounts of rebels scattered across the globe would remember and me, I would remember, I would remember everything.

"Three minutes."

"Remember the full level on all of them, no medium or small, they have to forget everything to do with those machines. We don't want any memories of how to make those monstrosities popping back into anyone's head."

"Two minutes," Taroff sounded. "Starting the program now."

I looked at the digital clock pressed into the wall, whereas everyone else was looking at Taroff, I was looking at the clock, counting down the seconds and minutes. He did it with time to spare.

"There, now we just wait."

"Right. Pete, Henry, come with me, it's time to help destroy those machines. We're meeting up with another group, come on, you three stay here and meet us when the programme's fully loaded."

Jason and the others walked out, turning their heads to watch the computer screen as they did so. Ten seconds before it all started, before the world forgot, forgot everything. I could see it all now, the world bathed in a golden light, flashing off every window into the eyes of laughing children, singing, drawing, learning. I was high on the building, standing on the tip of the ledge and looking over the world and all of the countries in it, turning to see a golden light spread across the entire world. Its beauty was even more glorious than what Jake had shown me before. But then the building sank and I fell down with it, when I got up from the rubble and gasping dust ,my friends surrounded me and one by one they each died in their own extraordinary ways; Jasper, Ruby, Chris, Sophie, Luke, Rose, Lucy and then Henry, but Henry wasn't dead and neither was Jake. Jake lay at my feet still, his ash-mauve eyes glazed over staring at the black world above. I fell down to my knees and cried, then, someone picked me up, it was Alec. His black eyes glazed over and he threw me down and pounced at me. I jolted from the world that had to be imagination, my memories swirling into nightmares, and I watched the clock again. It was five minutes past twelve, the people would be hooked up for another twenty five minutes. This new world really would be much better than the previous one, no more pointless murders to benefit those brain-hungry slaughterers, no more wasted lives. It really would be a perfect, golden world, but it wouldn't be for me, not with such viscous memories haunting me, *wherever I go they will always haunt me, always.*

"Hook me up to the machine."

"What?" It was Taroff who first spoke; Jake's expression told me that he was too stunned to believe my words.

"You can do it, right? You can put me on it, hook me up and I'll be just like everyone else, oblivious to the past, I'll forget everything."

"Well, everything to do with Talent School, it would be like remembering a normal boarding school."

"So, I'd still remember the deaths."

"Technically, yes, you'd just remember them differently."

"And Alec?" He didn't know who Alec was but it didn't stop him from answering.

"Well, yes, you'd remember everything up to the last time you were on the machines."

"So, she wouldn't remember me?" Jake said.

"I saw you at the library, the alleyway, which was before I went on my last machine, and when I was taken, I was put on them then."

"Yes, but you'd remember a normal boarding school, a normal world where you'd get your name on the cover if you published a book and where you wouldn't try and change the world, therefore that wouldn't have happened, so you wouldn't remember me."

"Could you make me forget?" I looked back towards Taroff. "About the deaths I mean, and Alec."

"Well, yes, I suppose, yes, most definitely."

"Can you do it?"

"Well, yes, but…" he looked over to Jake and he nodded in response.

"Yes, then," I prompted.

"Yes," he agreed.

Taroff began to work on a computer that was different from the rest, he took out one of the neck braces attached to the machine and checked it thoroughly.

"Jake," he was looking down at the floor, shuffling his feet, I knew his face was sombre. "Can you do one more thing for me?"

"Anything," he looked up and met my eyes, this was the last time I would get to see his sweet, powdered, ash-mauve eyes and the last time he would see my emerald green eyes, the colour of my eyes and not my name.

"Will you find some way to move my family back to the old house, as I thought they were there before anyway? Make them think they were always there and place me in the house to wake up in, can you do that? Is there any way you can do that?"

He smiled, this was the last time I would get to see him smile, I would miss his smile I would miss everything about him. "Yes, I should be able to. Taroff, you can set it to different levels, right?"

"Yes."

"Tanya, will you let me set it to medium?" He stroked my face, the last time he would ever touch me, "Will you let me be in your dreams?"

I shook my head with tears trickling as I did so. "If you're in my dreams then those deaths and Alec… it will all be in my nightmares, I have to forget. I have to forget everything, Jake, and I have to forget you."

"It's ready," Taroff pulled a seat around to where he held the neck brace and I sat down and felt the cold metal encase my neck. I never thought the feeling that I had hated so much would be so pleasurable, to know that this was the last time I would ever feel one of these things strangling my neck. I would never have to remember those terrible memories again, all the deaths would be gone; Jasper, Chris, Ruby, Malic… I wouldn't remember any of them and I didn't want to. The memories of Alec would be gone forever and Jake would be gone forever, Jake. *I love you, Jake, and I don't want to forget you, you are the only thing I do not want to forget, Jake, my angel.*

"Programme will start in ten seconds."

*No, why am I doing this, I have to get out, **ten**. Yet, I can't, my body feels numb and everything is starting to go black, I can feel myself slipping into a dream, **nine**. Jake is beside me but the world is going dark, I can't see anything, **eight**. No, for God's sake, no, **seven**. I have to remember, for God's sake, no, **six**. I want to remember you, Jake, get me off this thing, please, **five**. There has to be a way out of this and a way to still remember Jake, **four**. I can't sleep without you, I can't think or breathe without you, **three**. For God's sake, no, because there is a God and I know* *there is,* **two**. *There is a God because he sent me a saviour, a hero, he sent me an angel, he sent me Jake, my angel,* **one**.

"Jake, I love you." *Please let him hear it, don't let it just be in my head, in my thoughts; I love you, Jake, my angel, I love you.* "Jake, I love you."

"I love you, too, Tanya…"

# Epilogue

The summer holidays will be ending soon and as I sit here on the bench that often sparks my imagination for writing, I feel uneasy, as if something is not right in the world, yet everything seems the same. Except... one thing that is shaking me a bit, why is the house next to ours for sale? I don't remember it being for sale. Why would Mr McRiner sell his house? At his age he should stay where he is, no... wait... it isn't for sale, it's sold and there are people moving into it.

I should probably see who they are, after all, they might be freaks so I should definitely check this out. Just two people it would seem and no help in carrying things in, two boys, they look like brothers, one seems around my age and one seems older. One's walking over here, he must have spotted me, he must think I'm spying on them. His hair is jet black and his skin is pale, he has such strange features, features that are handsome and would leave a lasting impression on anyone. As he gets closer I can make out his eyes, the most amazing eyes I have ever seen, eyes that are a sweet, powdered, ash-mauve colour, they're beautiful; I swear I've seen those eyes before. He's wearing jeans, a black leather jacket and a black top to match, and a dog tag necklace with two, no, three tags on it.

"Hi, guess I'm you're new neighbour," he just smiled. He has such a charming smile, his teeth are so white, like the kind movie stars have, except not overdone.

"Oy? Come help me move these boxes," his brother is shouting.

"Hi," finally words. "I'm Tanya, Tanya Greyner."

"Hi, Tanya," his hand's going forward, oh, of course, how stupid of me, a handshake, "I'm Jake."

"Oy?" his brother is still shouting.

184

"I better go, I'll see you round," his voice is like caramel, it ripples through the air and around my ears.

"Yeah." Jake, it's such a lovely name, I don't know why but I like that name, it reminds me of something, a warm feeling, and I like it, no… I love it.